BUILD

UNIVERSES

William A. Pollard

Lucky, or What…?

© 2024 **Europe Books**| London
www.europebooks.co.uk | info@europebooks.co.uk

ISBN 9791220148665
First edition: March 2024

Edited by Stella Fusca

Lucky, or What…?

To Mark

There is light at the end of the tunnel.

Acknowledgements

My thanks to my publishing team at Europe Books for all the help and guidance they have given to me during the publishing process of this book. Their endeavours have produced an attractive and readable storey that will, perhaps, one day be a best seller.

I would also like to thank Sheila, my wife of over fifty-three years, for her patience and guidance during my cogitations over the storey line.

Copyright © William A. Pollard 2024
The right of William A. Pollard to be identified as author of
this work has been asserted in accordance with sections 77 and 78 of the Copyright, Designs and Patents Act 1988.

All Rights Reserved

This is a work of fiction. Names, characters, businesses, places, events and incidents are either the products of the author's imagination or used in a fictitious manner. Any resemblance to actual persons, living or dead, or actual events is purely coincidental.

No reproduction, copy or transmission of this publication may be made without written permission.
No paragraph of this publication may be reproduced, copied or transmitted save with
the written permission of the publisher,
or in accordance with the provisions
of the Copyright Act 1956
(as amended).

Any person who commits any
unauthorised act in relation to
this publication may be liable to criminal prosecution and civil claims for damage.

TABLE OF CONTENTS

PROLOGUE 17

PART 1 21
THE FINAL EIGHT 21

CHAPTER 1 23
   Jack Johnson & John Jackson 23
CHAPTER 2 27
   Jack's Luck 27
CHAPTER 3 35
   John's Luck 35
CHAPTER 4 41
   William Arthur & Arthur Williams.......................41
CHAPTER 5 47
   Arthur (Art) Williams' Luck..................................47
CHAPTER 6 53
   William (Billy) Arthur's Luck...............................53
CHAPTER 7 63
   Back to Art's Luck 63
CHAPTER 8 73
   June Gracey and Sister Gracey June 73
CHAPTER 9 79
   Sister Gracey June's Luck 79
CHAPTER 10 87
   June Gracey's Luck 87
CHAPTER 11 97
   Enzo Lorenzo & Lorenzo Enzo.............................97
CHAPTER 12 101
   Enzo (Eni) Lorenzo's Luck.................................101
CHAPTER 13 109
   Lorenzo (Lory) Enzo's Luck...............................109

PART 2 119
THE GAME 119

CHAPTER 14 121
   The Gamble 121
CHAPTER 15 129
   Nun's Revenge -v- Smelly Pants 129
CHAPTER 16 141
   Doom's Cloak -v Sweetness 141
CHAPTER 17 155
   Jumping Jack -v- Lover Boy 155
CHAPTER 18 171
   Big Willy -v- Black Hood 171
CHAPTER 19 191
   Lover Boy -v- Nun's Revenge 191
CHAPTER 20 213
   Sweetness -v- Black Hood 213
CHAPTER 21 235
   The Final Round 235
   Nun's Revenge -v- Black Hood 235
CHAPTER 22 251
   A Contract 251

EPILOGUE 257

PROLOGUE

You've just heard about some bloke winning a million quid.

So, what's the first thing that most people would think about that win…?

'*You lucky sod!*' Yes?

Perhaps that bloke won it from one of his premium bonds. It doesn't matter. Maybe he won it playing bingo. No, that doesn't matter. He could even have won it betting on the horses. That doesn't matter, either. What does matter is that the guy has just used up a substantial portion of the good luck that has been allocated to him… And when his allocated portion of good luck finally runs out he's in trouble, because all that he has to look forward to is his allocation of bad luck until, that is, his portion of good luck is reset and re-allocated to him.

So how does this work? Well, bear with me and you'll see how it works in a moment.

Next question – Who allocates all this good luck and bad luck?

The answer to that question is, 'Nobody knows.'

Actually that's not exactly true. The unseen, unknown entity – that's what we'll call it from now on – the entity that allocates one's luck is the thing…? being…? body…? unit …? call it what you will, it's the thing that allocates and manages luck. No living person has ever seen it. No living person ever will. All that needs to be understood is that when your good luck runs out you need to duck and weave to avoid your bad luck, until Entity has the time, or inclination, to re-set your good luck.

It can't be an easy job managing luck. Entity has to keep an eye on the level of luck (good or bad) remaining for each and every person in the world. That's a lot of people.

Don't forget, also, that creatures have good luck and bad luck, and there's a lot of creatures in the world. For example, it's bad luck when a snail is minding its own business lazily sliding across a patio to feed on a delicious looking lettuce leaf, and someone walks out of the conservatory and stands on its shell. We've all heard that ominous crunch of a snail's shell, haven't we? That person could have watched where he was walking, couldn't he? He would have seen the snail and avoided crushing its shell, but he wasn't paying attention and now the snail has lost its home and probably its life. To add insult to injury, the person will probably blame the snail for getting squashed!

Anyway, I digress.

The entity has one hell of a job making sure that everyone, and everything, in the world gets a share of both good and bad luck. The database for this must be huge. Enormous. And there must be quite a large team controlling the allocations - I bet they get really hot under the collar where they work.

So, next time you have a bit of good luck don't crow about it 'cos your run of good luck is being depleted. How quickly that depletion happens depends on the amount of good luck you experience in any one event. Winning a million pounds will deplete a lot of your good luck pretty quickly because it is, after all, a lot of good luck to get through. If, on the other hand you find a one pound coin on the pavement, that's a little bit of good luck and your depletion rate is slower.

Conversely, If you're having some bad luck take heart, because your quotient of bad luck is now being depleted and you'll soon be smiling again when your quotient of good luck has been re-set. Again, depending on the volume of bad luck in any one event, your bad luck is depleted accordingly.

Get the drift?

Something I should clarify for you; luck isn't as predetermined as Entity would have you believe. It is not set in concrete, stable, unchanging. Just because one is entwined in a run of bad luck it doesn't mean to say that one will not have any good luck at all. Luck isn't that cut and dry. Entity's systems allow one to mix and match luck to make life more balanced. After all, if one had absolutely *nothing* but bad luck I guess that that person would quickly expire. Perish. Die. Cease to exist.

Likewise, it is not possible for anyone to have absolutely nothing but good luck. If that happened, a person would live forever because good luck would prevent that person's death.

So some balance in luck must exist, so as to balance one's life. Entity is aware of that so has built some adjustments into its systems to create that balance in life.

Shall we see how all this works?

PART 1

THE FINAL EIGHT

CHAPTER 1

Jack Johnson & John Jackson

Jack Johnson is forty-five years old and is married with two children. He is a tech entrepreneur with a few million quid in his expanding bank account. With his really expensive silk underpants - which he wears only once - he owns the most expensive car ever made, wears the most expensive suits, walks around in the most expensive shoes and tells the time with the most expensive watch.

He owns and lives in a huge ten bedroomed house in an extremely desirable part of central London. His wife, April, is an ex-model. She's absolutely gorgeous. His eldest child, Jack junior, is in his final year of university with unquestionable prospects of leaving with a 'first'. Jack junior has thoughts on being an astronaut and there is every reason to believe that he will be the youngest astronaut to pilot a spaceship to some far-off planet. Jack senior's daughter, Ophelia, has just started university and is destined to be an Engineer.

Now don't go thinking that Jack senior has worked his fingers to the bone all his life to achieve such a comfortable and successful lifestyle. He hasn't. Something out there in the dark matter has organised and manipulated his life for him and is watching, with eager anticipation, Jack's quota of good luck being depleted. With all the good luck that Jack has had throughout his life he will soon know what it's like to experience bad luck.

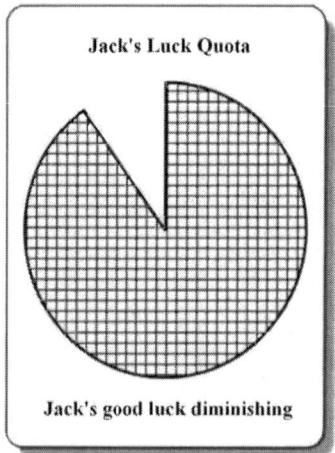 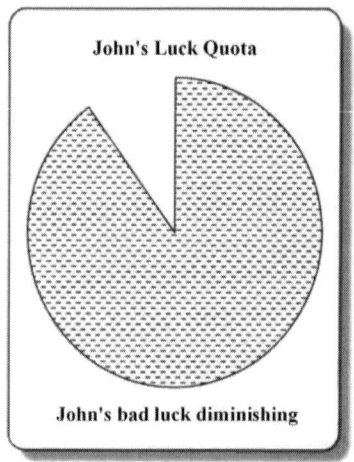

We'll see how his luck changes in a moment.

*

John Jackson, on the other hand, has led a somewhat miserable existence since he was born.

He must have had every ailment known to mankind in his younger years, but he rode through those times to reach his present age of forty-five years. He presently lives in a rented two bedroomed house in Margate, and he used to be a bin collector for the council. A respected job worth doing, with a liveable wage (just), regular hours and a decent lunch break.

His wife, Mavis, works at a checkout in the local supermarket and his son, Bert, stacks the shelves at the same outlet. Mavis got him that job as soon as he left school, and Bert – not an abbreviation of Bertram, or Albert, or Herbert, not an abbreviation of anything, it's just the name his parents gave him - Bert enjoys the responsibility placed on his shoulders from such an important role. John's daughter had been the daughter from hell, and John was bloody glad that she upped and went to live with some waster in a squat somewhere on the outskirts of Sheffield.

John once enjoyed the tea and cakes brought out to him for elevenses by an appreciative housewife during his rounds. Not anymore. He dropped a bin on his bin collection lorry driver's foot, putting the driver into hospital for a month and making him unemployable as a lorry driver for the rest of his life. Now that's what you might call 'bad luck…' Or perhaps not.

Anyway, the driver sued the firm for negligence and received a massive pay-out in compensation. Enough for the guy to retire to Spain and live in palatial comfort without having to work ever again. This did not please the firm's CEO. In fact, when John's CEO found out that the driver was now lounging by a pool in the sun at the firm's expense, he was furious.

The CEO's anger was passed down the line to John's Supervisor, with orders to take appropriate action.

So, when all the bin lorries return to the depot, and they tip their loads out of their arses onto the floor of the enclosed yard to be sorted, John's whole day is now one miserable round of sweeping the loose detritus into a pile so that a man sat on a comfortable seat in a bulldozer can push the pile further into the enclosure. John doesn't even get the privilege of sorting the rubbish into the 'useful' or 'not useful' receptacles.

John really does have to work his fingers to the bone to scrape out a meagre living. At least his wife and son each get a discount on the weekly shop.

CHAPTER 2

Jack's Luck

Jack is presently enjoying life. Things couldn't be better.

He needs to start looking over his shoulder.

Entity has just run a check on Jack's good luck quota and has noticed that it is ninety-five percent depleted. It won't be long before Jack's lifelong run of good luck runs out… And then he will have to start ducking and weaving until Entity re-sets it.

Jack's just had the 'heads up' from a reliable secret source about an investment that is too good to miss. An opportunity to double his money with a 'dead cert' investment without even getting up off his chair.

It is a tip on some shares being issued by a company that is 'on the up', as indicated by Jack's stock market insider. He should, according to this source, invest heavily because these shares are 'certain to triple in value within the next six months.' So Jack ploughed almost a third of his company's liquid assets into these attractive sounding company shares. That's a lot of money, but so what? This investment is going to make a pile of the stuff when those company shares 'triple in weight,' to quote his reliable source. Lucky, eh? From tips made by this reliable source Jack has made several such investments in the past, and they have *all* made him a shed load of cash. With a source this reliable what can possibly go wrong? Jack sat back, smugly smiling from ear-to-ear.

The telephone on his desk chimed. It was his trusted Finance Director. This guy is an accountant of the highest order. He has steered Jack's business from one good financial call to the next. He has never, ever, let Jack down with his valued opinions and advice.

"Jack, have you got a couple of minutes some time to come round for a chat? I've got something you should see."

"Sure," replied Jack, looking in his diary. "I'm tied up for about a week. Can we meet up then?"

"No probs, but don't leave it too long. I've got a small window on this opportunity".

Jack completed his application for the company shares and waited for a reply from the invested company. As soon as confirmation of his purchase was sent to him, he printed off his acknowledgement and gathered up the paperwork to give to his Finance Director. After shutting down his PC he made his way home, smugly thinking what a good boy he had been to make the company so much money.

The following week, as per their arranged meeting, Jack gently knocked on his Finance Director's door and entered the office without waiting for permission. Not that he needed permission to enter the office, he always knocked out of politeness.

"Hi Jack. Thanks for coming round," welcomed the Finance Director.

"No problem, Peregrine. I had to come round, anyway, to give you this stuff." handing over the paperwork detailing Jack's transaction.

The finance manager looked over the documents and blew out a lungful of air through puffed out cheeks.

"That's a lot of money out of the company account, Jack. Shouldn't you have had a word with me before making this purchase?"

Jack paused for thought, then answered, "I got the heads up from a reliable and trusted source. He's never let me down before."

"Well, I'll still run a few checks on the company, anyway, just to be safe. Not that any checks will do any good at this stage because it seems to me, from this paperwork, that it's a done deal."

"What was it you wanted to see me about," enquired Jack.

"Oh, yes. With the government's recent revision of the UK tax laws I thought we should get some of the firm's liquid assets out of their hands. My source tells me that there is an offshore account that provides some good returns. The bank account is tied to its country of origin, but the investment is safe because it is underwritten by that country's government. There is a guaranteed return of investment plus a tax-free fifteen percent profit per annum. What do you think?"

I don't know," answered Jack, "I always leave these things entirely in your hands, as you know," conveniently forgetting about the transaction he had recently made! "What do *you* think?"

"Well, I got the tip from an insider in the foreign government, so it must be legitimate information. I reckon we could invest, say, thirty percent now and draw on it as and when necessary."

"Sounds like a plan. Go for it."

The Finance Director put the appropriate steps in motion and before long received confirmation of the transaction.

*

Spoiler alert!

As soon as Jack had completed his transaction last week, regarding the company's share investment, he had used up all the remaining good luck that had been allocated to him.

Entity had heard an alarm bell ringing and looked into why the alarm had woken it from an afternoon nap. Interrogating its system, Entity noticed that Jack Johnson's good luck had been completely depleted by the share investment and so, in line with its own protocol for allocation of luck, it took appropriate steps to allocate Jack's good luck to someone else.

That someone was John Jackson, but we're getting ahead of ourselves, aren't we, because we've not heard how Jack's depletion of good luck affects him.

As soon as Entity established that Jack's good luck had run out, it started procedures to re-set Jack's luck. The first thing to address was Jack's share investment.

Entity decided that the company in which Jack had invested should go bust, so that company's share value immediately sank to an all-time low. Almost flat line on the chart.

A couple of days after Jack's investment arrived in that company's bank, the company's CEO had been found with his hand in the till and had been arrested. Auditors had been called in by the board and it was revealed that that company's profits had been frittered away by the CEO on fast cars, gambling, expensive holidays and loose women.

In actual fact, sale of that company's assets will not now, in any way, cover the debts clocked up by the CEO, so it went into liquidation. Creditors may recover about five pence in the pound, according to the newscast, but as a shareholder Jack has lost everything he invested.

When Jack heard about this, via the TV news desk, while munching away at his dinner one evening it's an understatement to say that he was gutted. His dinner tray flew across the room and splattered his lobster bisque all over the wall of the lounge, narrowly missing his wife, knocking over the parrot's cage and smashing several items of crockery that were part of his treasured dinner service, a gifted wedding present from his mum.

On his way to work the following morning he thought about how he could face his Finance Director with the bad news. His best line of defence, he decided, was to put the firm's loss down to a bit of bad luck and write it off the books. At least the firm won't have to pay as much corporation tax as it had done in the past.

Unfortunately, because his good luck had been completely depleted, he must now join the ranks of those in the bad luck bubble. So what happens next?

Do you remember the trusted Finance Director's advice? Well, Jack's bad luck affected the outcome of that particular investment. A mere few weeks after Peregrine had transferred a substantial amount of the firm's wealth to the offshore account, the country which owned the bank in which Peregrine had made the deposit froze all foreign transactions and investments, and closed the bank down. That country's government declared all the money in that bank as its own! Jack lost every penny that had been invested in this 'safe' bank, recommended by his trusted and reliable Finance Director, Peregrine.

There's an old adage which states 'It never rains, but it pours.' In Jack's case, a truer word was never said.

The transactions made by both Jack and Peregrine attracted a copious amount of attention from the UK authorities and a detailed investigation was carried out to identify if any money laundering had taken place. Although none was found, every social media page discussed Jack and his firm's dealings and some even accused him of allowing terrorist activity on his web site. This was a crushing blow to the firm's business and over a few weeks Jack eventually ran out of friends, ran out of support, ran out of money, and ran out of business. The stock market's growth line on Jack's business crashed through the floor into the basement.

In the process of trying to keep his firm afloat he used up all of his savings, and with no business or investments coming into his company Jack had no choice but to put the firm into the liquidator's hands.

Now that's just bad luck, Isn't it?

Or is it…?

CHAPTER 3

John's Luck

Guess What?

When Jack Johnson ran out of good luck, John Jackson's good luck quota was immediately replenished one hundred percent by Entity, and he is now ready to start cashing in on some of his good luck.

What do you reckon happens?

Well, for a start he got really fed up with being the compound sweeper-upper. It was a soul destroying job and his supervisor was perpetually on his back.

"You've missed a bit," or, "Can't you work any faster?" or, "You're not doing a good enough job," or, "Isn't it about time you got a new brush?" or even, "Why do you want a new brush?"

John was ready to punch this pig-faced, obnoxious bloke on the nose but thought better of it. The last thing he wanted was a criminal record for assault, but he had to do something to improve his lot. He applied for promotion. Didn't get it. He applied for a new position further along the food chain, an office job. Didn't get it.

Having exhausted all his options for a change at his present firm, there was just one path left for him to take. He would resign from this place and try the Job Centre to see what they had to offer.

One Monday morning his patience snapped. When he arrived at work he tore up his clocking-in card, threw the pieces into the face of his favourite supervisor, told the guy what he thought of him and walked out of the yard.

The supervisor followed John, shouting, "Get back in here and do your job, Jackson or I'll sack you right now! Come back, now!"

John didn't respond. He just kept walking until he reached the bus stop outside the yard's gates. Even so, the supervisor was hot on John's tail bellowing obscenities at him, but John just sat on the bench in the bus shelter until the bus arrived, arms folded, lips tightly shut, not responding to the tirade of abuse. He quietly boarded the bus, and when the bus doors closed John turned and looked through the window. In a final act of defiance he stuck two fingers up at the supervisor who was, by now, going mental at John's insolence.

'*What now?*' thought John. Out of a job with rent to find, bills to pay and a wife and son to clothe he pondered over his next move.

Mavis - Mave to those who knew her - was surprised to see John so early in the day. He told her what he had done and *she* then kicked off.

"What about the rent?"

"How are we going to pay the bills?"

"I'm never going to get that new dress, now, am I?"

Now, you would think that John was still in his bad luck bubble, wouldn't you? Not so.

John was beginning to think this really was the end of the world when an idea exploded inside his head. He walked out of the rented dump that he lived in and went straight downtown to his union office.

Normally one would have to make an appointment to see the union rep. After all, this union rep was constantly on the television in his Armani suit shouting the odds at the camera, telling anyone watching the news that, "…recent negotiations for a pay rise had broken down because the employer wouldn't meet us halfway," and, "It's time we took some action."

Not today, though. This union rep didn't have any TV interviews to attend, and none of his members had complained about anything of note recently. So he sat in his office, lightly drumming his fingers on his desk and waiting for something to happen so that he had something to do.

His telephone rang. "There's a mister Jackson in reception, sir. He hasn't made an appointment but he asks if he can see you," said his secretary, who doubled as a receptionist.

After a pause for thought the union rep answered, "Okay, send him in."

John entered the room, was invited to sit and the union rep asked what he could do for him. John spent the next thirty-five minutes giving the rep chapter and verse on why he had walked out of his job. To much tutting and cheek puffing the rep took notes, interrupted John occasionally to ask a question and finally dropped his pen onto the pad he was writing on.

"Well, John, I think we have sufficient grounds to introduce you to the union's legal beagle because I'm confident that the firm is guilty of constructive dismissal."

This was music to John's ears. His luck was now, he thought, turning in his direction… And about time, too.

Over the next few months John capitalised on as much of the good luck, allocated to him by Entity, as he could.

For a start, a crowd funding page on social media, together with a grant from the union's funds, raised several thousand pounds to help with John's present day-to-day expenses. At the same time the publicity raised by John's union made him into quite a celebrity, with TV interviews, offers from local shops, and parcels from the many food banks surrounding his home. Even his wife's employer, a local supermarket, gave Mave a salary rise, with free vegetables for as long as she worked there, and his son was promoted from stock mover to stock taker.

John was soon offered a job as a warehouse stock manager and could eventually afford a modest mortgage. His wife was promoted to supervisor at the supermarket and to top it all, his union solicitor won his constructive dismissal challenge and John was awarded several hundred thousand pounds in compensation. He could even loan his daughter a couple of thousand pounds when she came begging for money… Not that he would ever get any of it back.

John's luck really had turned a corner and, just as Jack Johnson's run of bad luck continued for several more years, so did John Jackson's run of good luck.

Now that's what you call good luck.

Or is it…?

CHAPTER 4

William Arthur & Arthur Williams

Are you lucky in love? Some men are, some men aren't.

Two boys, William Arthur and Arthur Williams… To minimise any confusion shall we call them 'Billy' and 'Art'? So, two boys, Billy and Art, and one girl; that combination doesn't always work, does it? Much to these two boys' naivety, one is about to strike it lucky, while the other will wish he lived on another planet, because the entity is watching their luck levels very closely. An alarm has brought it to Entity's attention that the luck quotas for these two boys are approaching a re-set.

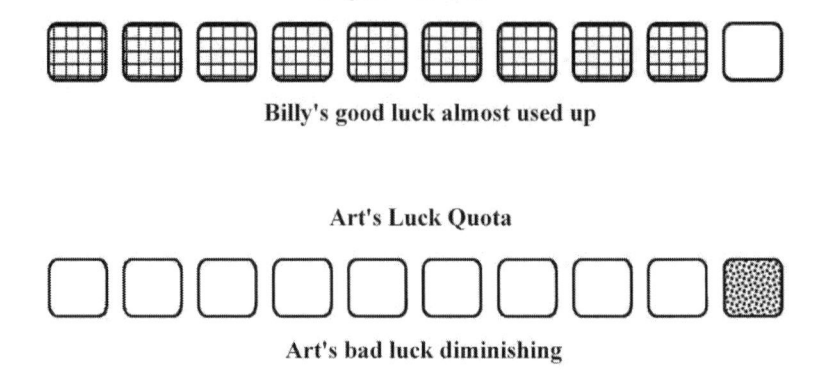

Billy's Luck Quota

Billy's good luck almost used up

Art's Luck Quota

Art's bad luck diminishing

Billy and Art go to the same school.

They are both sixteen and a bit years old – ahh, memories – they are in the same class at school and they do absolutely everything together. They are best friends... At the moment.

They've both taken their GCSE's and are now studying for their 'A' Levels. Billy's GCSE results were outstanding, which is not surprising because he is a whizz-kid at everything. He excels in sport, he didn't cause a fire in the science lab, his cooking skills are on a par with the most renowned chefs, and several of the girls in his class – in fact in the school – think he's a dreamboat and fantasise about the day he will pay for them to sit with him in the back row of the cinema. Actually, a couple of the older girls would probably pay for *him* to sit in the back row of the cinema with them, just for the privilege of having their bra size measured by his roving hands! He is, to them, perfect in every way.

His parents are filthy rich and both have high-powered jobs in the city, and Billy now has a brand new state of the art motorbike bought by them as a 'Well done' for getting good GCSE results. They have plans for which university they will pay for him to attend, and Billy has already been introduced to some of the country's top employers in preparation for him leaving the corridors of learning to become a Captain of industry.

He's got it made... At the moment.

*

Art isn't quite so lucky.

Art's parents are typical salt-of-the-earth working class grafters, always striving to make ends meet and provide for Art. Don't get me wrong on this. There is absolutely nothing wrong with being a salt-of-the-earth working class grafter. The vast majority of parents are just that, but not every family can be as lucky as Billy's family.

Art's dad is a lorry driver, always on some trip driving his boss's articulated truck. He doesn't have to load the truck, that's down to whatever depot he's parked up in to collect the load for delivery. He does, however, have to get his load safely to its destination in one piece, and that could mean many hours travelling to and from the continent. He is very rarely at home, but when he is he spends his time down on his allotment.

Art's mum is a hospital cleaner, a most important job and one that commands respect from the best of surgeons.

Art didn't do so well with his GCSE's. He barely scraped passes in his exams to keep him at school to study for his 'A' levels, but neither Art nor his parents hold out much hope of him going to university. They are all of the opinion that even if he did get into a university he probably wouldn't be able to stick it out because, sadly, he, '… just doesn't have it in him.' However, in true grafting tradition, he'll give it a good go and see what happens.

*

With regard to girls, both boys really fancy the same girl in their class. Nobody else. Just that one girl. The rest of the girls are plain in comparison to this one, and the two boys frequently partake in plenty of shower exercise at home while fantasising over her.

Her name is Emma and all the boys in Art's class fancy their chances with her, although they have all yet to get past the hurdle of being accepted for a date. When asked, Emma usually plays the 'bad hair' card, or the 'I've got too much studying to do' card, or the 'Mum's asked me to babysit' card. Sometimes she plays the 'Get Lost!' card because she thinks that particular boy isn't handsome enough, or perhaps he smells or picks his nose or scratches his bum. Who knows? Anyway, she chooses any excuse not to have a date with the nerds.

Whilst she hangs out with her girl's crowd during school hours, she meets both Billy and Art at the gates at school chucking out time and she allows them both to walk her home, which isn't such a big deal because her house is on the way to the boys' homes, anyway. She probably likes the security of walking between the boys, arms around their waists, to fend off any possible approaches by the other boys.

As is usual in these situations both boys *think* that Emma fancies him more than the other. Also, as is usual in these situations, Emma is not letting on which one she fancies. She *thinks* they will come to an agreement over who will ask her for a date, one way or the other.

The entity will decide for them…

CHAPTER 5

Arthur (Art) Williams' Luck

Art has worshipped the ground on which Emma walks ever since he first met her.

Their secondary school is a mixed sex school, and in the first year Art and Emma were in separate classes. Nonetheless, he spotted her in the playground every lunch time and wished that he could muster the courage to approach her to ask for a date. From the second year onwards, however, the class organisers put the kids into classes that reflected their abilities. Art just made it into the 'better than them' class, but he knew it would be a struggle to keep up, 'cos his dad said so. He'd give it a try, anyway. What has he got to lose? If he flunks his grades he can always join the salt-of-the-earth grafting society and be a lorry driver, like his dad.

On the first day of the new term he deliberately picked a desk next to a window at the back of the class. That way he could see everyone, especially Emma, he could daydream out of the window during the boring lessons and he stood a good chance of not being picked to answer any questions from the teacher. That role was open to all the know-it-all's that sat at the front, hoping to be picked to answer questions by the teacher.

Emma didn't sit with the know-it-all's. She sat in the centre of the class where she could distance herself sufficiently to not be called a know-it-all, but at the same time be in a position to be noticed and admired by the boys. After a couple of weeks she sort of charmed her way into Billy and Art's bubble, more to be seen with them than anything else, and the three of them spent a lot of out-of-school time together.

After a while, it became clear to the boys that they allowed her into the bubble for very different reasons. Billy's motives were far from honourable, but Art just wanted to be next to her, to be ready to defend her from whatever Billy had in mind for her. Art was in love with Emma. Billy was in love with himself.

So Emma's bread was buttered on both sides. On the one hand she was admired by many of the girls in school because she hung out with Billy, but on the other hand she knew that Art was always there to protect her because he had once told her that.

One sunny day towards the end of the school year Billy's good luck quota bottomed out. The reason for that will be explained in a moment. Having said that, Art's bad luck quota had not quite peaked, so Entity couldn't reset his life's luck quota immediately. It had to wait until Art had had his fill of bad luck, which wasn't too far in the future.

Billy wasn't at school that day. His mum had telephoned the school secretary to let her know that Billy '...Won't be in today,' and that she '...would make sure that he did his homework in time for him to return to school.'

At last! Art would enjoy his walk home with Emma. Just the two of them with nobody else to get in the way. This was a good opportunity to make a gentle move on her without Billy getting in the way or making any derogatory comments about him.

Billy did that all the time, make derogatory comments about Art, just so that he would look good in front of everyone else. Art suffered this ignominy because when he and Billy were away from the crowd Billy wasn't a bad person. He was a good pal at those times, and anyway, derogatory comments or not, when he was with Billy they were both always surrounded by girls.

When the bell sounded for 'end of lessons' Art made his way to the school gates, as was his and Billy's usual routine, to wait for Emma. Girls always found something to do or talk about before making their way home, didn't they? So Art played the waiting game until Emma bored of her discussions about boys, or dads, or body weight, or the size of one's boobs, or whatever girls secretly discuss in a group, until she skipped to the gates to be welcomed by him.

Today, Emma was not alone when she approached the gates. She noticed that Art was on his own and her heart skipped a beat.

She was surrounded by six or seven other girls, some in the same class as her. Art thought *'Now that's just* bad luck, isn't it? I hope they all push off somewhere.' Art's bad luck quota moved round a notch and was now showing ninety-nine point nine-eight recurring percent bad luck depleted. Entity didn't move from his console. He needed to be on hand to reset Art's life's luck quota when the present level of bad luck reached one hundred percent depleted. He had already reset Billy's.

The group of girls approached the gates where Art stood patiently waiting for Emma to arrive. When they eventually converged there was a lot of sniggering and secret whispers but Art ignored that and waited for Emma to come forward. When she looped arms with Art the girls all laughed behind hands that hid their mouths, their faces turned down in mock humiliation. Art didn't know what to make of this joviality so he unhooked himself from Emma's grip, threw her hand away and stormed off, not wanting to hear what the girls were saying about him. His bad luck quota moved another notch to ninety-nine point nine-nine recurring percent bad luck.

With steam shooting out of his ears he stomped his way down the road. He sure as hell refused to stand there and be made to look like a love-stricken fool. If Emma was so much against him she can just go and jump in the lake.

Emma was alarmed at Art's brusque departure. As Art kicked at the grass on his way from the crowd she could see that he was upset and angry. She turned to the crowd of girls, now laughing heartily at Art's embarrassment, and shouted, "Shut up!" A deathly silence descended on the girls who all stood and watched Emma chase after Art.

Catching up to him she yanked his jacket sleeve to bring him to a halt and asked, "Wait, what's wrong?"

With less steam escaping from Art's ears he straightened his back, took a deep breath and answered, "I'm fed up with being the butt of everybody's jokes. Billy doesn't waste one second in making snide comments about me in front of you and everyone just to make him look good, and now all the girls are following his lead. I've had enough of it, Emma. I *was* going to ask you to go to the pictures with me, but seeing as how you think I'm a joke just forget it. Go get your laughs elsewhere."

He left Emma stood in the middle of the pavement in shock. She had never been spoken to like that before and it wasn't nice. Tears rolled down her cheeks as she watched Art make his way home. After a few minutes she wiped her nose on her sleeve and made her way to her own home… Alone for once, and that didn't feel nice either.

On his way down the street Art crossed the road and tripped up on the kerb. Splat! He fell face down and muddied his school blazer and trousers. Mum wasn't going to be too pleased that she now had a cleaning job to do before his next visit to school, tomorrow, but that was just Art's bad luck, wasn't it?

He couldn't help wondering when his luck would change…

*

Art's bad luck quota clicked round to one hundred percent depleted, squawking an alarm in the entity's system.

'About time, too.' thought the entity as he reset Art's life's luck quota level.

CHAPTER 6

William (Billy) Arthur's Luck

Let's leave Art for a moment to see how Billy's change of luck changed his life.

You may recall that Billy's good luck quota was slowly being depleted. For a while it levelled off at zero point two percent remaining. Now that's not a lot in comparison to a lifetime of good luck. Like it, or not, Billy's good luck was slowly ebbing away and it would soon be fully depleted. He didn't know it, but he was about to find out.

*

A couple of weeks before Art lost his temper with Emma, a Saturday, Billy was asked by his mum if he would go to the shop to get some more carrots and potatoes so that she could make dad's favourite tea, meat and potato pie. She gave Billy a five-pound note and suggested that he could put the change into his savings tin if he wanted to, knowing that he would probably spend the change on sweets.

Enjoying the warm sun on his way to the shops his thoughts centred on the pick-and-mix goodies that he could now buy. Lucky, eh? Up ahead he saw Michael, one of the boys from his class. As the two boys approached each other he noticed that Michael was scratching his arm.

"Hiya Billy." welcomed Michael.

"Hi, Mike. Got anything going on?" This was the usual greeting by boys that meet in the street.

"Nah. Just been to see Aunty May about this rash," volunteered Mike, rolling up his shirt sleeve. "She says it's measles, so I can't go to school until it's gone. I've got to stay at home."

"Wow! That's a bit of rotten luck, isn't it?"

"Nah! I'm going to miss R.E. on Monday" smiled Mike with his palms turned upwards. "Do you want it? It itches a bit, but it's worth it to miss R.E." holding out his arm.

"Nah. If I get it, it'll leave Art on his own to make a move on Emma, and I want to get in there before he does. Anyway, I've been picked for the school's county athletics team and we've got a tournament coming up."

"Emma. Wow! She's a cracker. She's perfect in every way known to man. Do you think you'll succeed?"

"Yeah, no problem. She fancies me like hot chocolate, but Art's always hanging around so she plays it cool with us. If Art was out of the way she'd cave in to me like I was the only bloke on earth. Every time she looks at me I just know that she can't wait to get her hands inside my trousers. When she sees me perform at the athletics I bet she'll be wrapped around me like an octopus, and you know what? She'll do absolutely *anything* I want."

"I'll knock on Art's door tomorrow and see if I can give this to him," suggested Mike, holding his arm aloft with a grin.

"Thanks, pal. I owe you for that." Billy held out his hand to shake Mike's hand.

The boys parted company. Billy continued his journey to the shops.

Mike never did pay a visit to Art.

Entity saw an opportunity here, but had to bide its time until Billy's good luck was completely depleted.

As Billy approached the shop he saw a two-pound coin glinting at him in the sunlight. It was about ten feet in front of him and several people stood on it without even noticing what it was. Billy focused on the coin, willing the pedestrians not to see it.

"It's mine, it's mine, its mine," he repeated to himself as he got closer to the coin. And the coin *was* his when he finally reached its location and bent down to pick it up.

"Fantastic luck!" he beamed.

Was it…?

Billy's good luck had now run out and his life's luck quota required an immediate reset.

Entity obliged and pounced…

Billy entered the grocer's shop and picked out a bag of potatoes and a bag of carrots.

After queuing to pay for his goods he delved into his right hand trouser pocket for Mum's five pound note. It wasn't there. Dropping the potatoes and carrots onto the counter he delved into his left hand trouser pocket. The fiver wasn't there either, but the two pound coin was. A queue of people waiting to pay for their goods began to form behind him.

Frantically searching all his pockets for the fiver it eventually dawned on him that it was well and truly lost. Some obstreperous person in the now long queue muttered "What the hell is he doing?" Billy looked round to see a field of hostile faces, all wanting to go somewhere other than this shop.

With a huff of exasperation he banged the two-pound coin on the counter. The shop assistant sat in front of him, staring blankly at his face. Someone else shouted "Get a move on!" from somewhere at the back of the queue, now snaking down one aisle and up the next. A little boy opened the bag of crisps that his mum had not yet paid for and a bloke delved into his bag of grapes to pass the time.

"What's wrong?" Billy asked the shop assistant.

"That's not enough," she answered, nodding to the potatoes and carrots.

Billy had an executive decision to make. Does he put the potatoes back, or does he put the carrots back. The shop assistant made Billy's mind up for him. She took the carrots off the counter and dropped them into a basket lounging by her feet. Cashing up the cost of the potatoes she reached into the cash drawer and took out a ten-pence piece, the change from the two-pound coin Billy had slapped onto the counter. Picking up the spuds, he left the shop to the cheers of the queue of people waiting to be served.

Arriving home he had to 'fess up to mum about losing the fiver. She wasn't pleased, but she could, '… make do,' with what she had. She took back the ten-pence change on the basis that Billy hadn't done a proper job.

A doleful Billy left the kitchen to watch some TV.

*

About ten days later, on a Thursday, Billy felt really rough. He woke up with a fever and a runny nose. His throat felt like it had a roll of barbed wire wedged in it and he had a hacking dry cough. He had a massive headache 'cos he didn't sleep all that well last night … And he had a really irritating itch behind his ear.

Mum looked inside his mouth and saw an outbreak of little white spots on the inside of his cheeks.

"No going out for you my boy. Looks like you've got the measles."

Billy could not believe his luck.

On the following Monday, the day Art had his row with Emma, Billy laid in bed scratching everywhere he could reach. His measles rash had appeared with a vengeance.

This measles thing was a real blow to Billy. For a start, he had missed the athletics meeting. He had trained hard for months to show off his speed to the county's selectors and he had broken the county record for both the two-hundred and four hundred metre sprints right there in front of them. Although he earned a place in the county team, this had now been taken up by Jonny Postlethwaite in class 4B because Billy was a prisoner at home.

Next, he was beating himself up trying not to think about Art and Emma. What were they saying about him? Where were they going? What were they *doing*?

His mum told him, "It's no good pining after Emma. If she likes you, she will show it in good time."

Some consolation that was. Anyway, he wasn't 'pining after her.' He was annoyed that Art had been presented with a free run at her and would, by now, have sampled the delights of Emma's assets before him.

On Tuesday, Mum gently knocked on his bedroom door and entered with his lunch time tray. "You've got some mail," she advised, placing the tray in Billy's lap. "Mike's collected your exam results from school for you."

Billy tore open the envelope staring up at him from the tray. This was the news he had been waiting for since last Easter. This envelope held the results of his 'A' level exams. Ignoring the toast in front of him he read the letter, then sat back and stared at the wall. Mum had waited silently by the door while he read the contents of the envelope.

"Well?" she asked. "Tell me what you got." She obviously knew it was the exam results because she saw where the letter was from, this being printed on the back of the envelope.

Billy didn't answer. His mum came into the bedroom and sat on the edge of Billy's bed.

"Are you going to show me?" she prompted.

Billy screwed the letter up and threw it away. Mum retrieved it, flattened it out and silently read its contents.

"It's not too bad Billy. They're not all A's ... ," '*or even B's,*' she thought, "but they will get you a place in another University."

"They're rubbish!" retorted Billy. "They won't get me into the Uni that counts." He bent his head down in utter misery.

'*What bloody rotten luck,*' Billy thought.

*

That Tuesday and the following Wednesday and Thursday were days of miserable self-pity for Billy, but on Friday he was cheered in the knowledge that Art was coming round to see him. The doctor had advised that he was not infectious anymore and he could have visitors without fear of passing on the virus. He was, nonetheless, still itching everywhere.

Art was shown into his bedroom by Mum and he sat on the side of the bed. Pleasantries over, Billy got straight to the point.

"How's Emma?"

"Oh, she's okay."

"Just okay? Is she coming to see me some time?"

"Doubt it, Billy. Your mum says you'll be up and running soon, then you'll see her yourself."

"Okay, so what's what?"

"What do you mean, 'What's what?'"

"What's what…? What have you two been up to?"

Billy was eager to know what Art and Emma had been '*doing*' while he had been confined to his bed.

"Oh, not a lot," offered Art, looking away so as to hide his face from Billy.

Billy stared at Art for a few seconds, trying to decide if Art was hiding something from him. He was surely acting that way.

"What…?" Billy demanded. "What you got to tell me?"

Art looked at Billy, took a deep breath and blurted out "Emma and me are an item…"

Billy screamed, "I knew it! I knew it! You just couldn't wait 'til I was out of the way, could you?"

"It's not like that Billy…"

Billy interrupted, "Get out! Piss off! Some pal you are."

Art stood and left the room in silence. He knew that he had just lost a friend, but he considered that that was his friend's loss, not his.

Billy cursed his bad luck. He will need to accept his fate and get used to having bad luck, because he will have bad luck for many years to come.

He didn't get a place at University. He got a place in a college of further education but he couldn't find a course that suited him and he flunked out in the second year.

He tried an apprenticeship. That didn't work, either. He didn't like getting his hands dirty.

He did, however, pass the HGV driving course and he now works as a lorry driver at Art's dad's firm.

Jog on, Billy. Your good luck quota will be replenished one day…

CHAPTER 7

Back to Art's Luck

So what happened to Art after his row with Emma?

Well, you'll recall that the entity had recently reset his life's luck quota to one hundred percent good luck, even though Art had lost his temper with Emma. He didn't know it yet, but he was about to taste the delights of good luck.

*

Monday, after school chucking out time.

Arriving home in a bit of a state 'cos he had tripped up and muddied his clothes, his mum looked him up and down and asked, "How on earth did you get into that state? You've got mud all down the front of your blazer and trousers."

"I just tripped up on my way home from school. I couldn't help myself. Sorry, Mum."

"Not to worry. Get yourself out of those clothes and I'll give them a scrub now so that they are dry for tomorrow. Have you been crying?" noticing Art's streaky cheeks where tears had run down them.

"Not really. I just had a row with Emma and her crowd. Those girls are really malicious with their inane comments and mickey-taking. They're always jibing at somebody and poking fun at them. I thought Emma was above that."

Remembering the time when she was Art's age, and the awkward way all kids suffered 'growing pains', she felt sorry for Art. He had enthusiastically told her, on numerous occasions, how much he liked Emma, and how much he enjoyed her company, and how much he wished he could be with her all the time. Art's mum always smiled at his enthusiasm over Emma as she remembered her own first love, but Art was hurting and she knew that it would take time for his hurt to heal.

"Go and get changed and we'll sit down and talk about it over a cup of tea." Sitting down with a cup of tea was always mum's answer to a problem.

After changing his clothes he returned to the kitchen where his cup of tea beckoned from the kitchen table.

"Tell me all about it," she prompted.

Art told her everything. He told her about the way Billy was always hanging around with Emma and himself, and about the way that Billy wanted Emma's body more than he did her friendship, and about the way that Billy talked about what he would do if he got her on her own. He told her that if Billy was out of the way a bit more he wouldn't feel so nervous about asking Emma out for a date.

With tears in his eyes Art went on to tell his mum about what happened at the school gates with Emma and her crowd and how the girls had hurt his feelings, "… but Emma didn't make any move to stop them taking the mickey. Well, Emma can just go and get lost! If she likes

Billy more than me then she can have him, and I don't care!"

Art's mum put her arm round his shoulders to comfort him. "Don't take it to heart, dear. I'm sure that Emma didn't want to embarrass you, but girls are like that, sometimes. They always look as if they're poking fun at you, but it's only bravado. They don't really mean it. They have to be like that so that they can score points while in a crowd, but most girls are entirely different on their own. In fact …" Mum continued, "most of the time they are like that to get your attention because they fancy you. I did that when I fancied a boy, and I ended up marrying him."

"But Emma's not 'most girls' and I'm pretty sure that none of them fancy me. Emma always meets Billy and me after school, not that lot. It's clear to me what she thinks of me as soon as Billy is not around. She obviously prefers to be with the crowd more than she does with me, and it's clear that I'm the spare part as far as Emma and Billy is concerned."

"I'm sure she doesn't think that, Art. Why don't you go round to her place to talk it out with her?"

"No chance. If she wants to talk, she can just jolly well come to me! I'm not going to give her, or that lot, the satisfaction of bowing and scraping in front of them."

Mum left Art to stare into his now empty cup. She was confident that he would find a way to repair his relationship with the love of his life. Art was like that, always finding a way out of a bad situation.

*

The entity had watched Art's performance with the girls after school and then with his mum when he got home.

It was all a bit puzzling to Entity because it knew that it had re-set Art's life's luck quota. So why wasn't Art having any good luck?

Was Entity losing control of his life's luck regulator? Was there a problem with it?

Entity carried out a system check to make sure that nothing was wrong and that his life's luck regulator still functioned properly. Nope, everything seems to work okay. So why hadn't Art's good luck kicked in? Perhaps it needed a push in the right direction? Entity knew just the thing to get Art's good luck put into first gear.

*

On Tuesday Art spent his day at school in his lonely bubble.

In class he didn't let on that he was still upset with Emma. He just ignored her. He acted as if she didn't exist, much to her unease. At lunch time, in the playground, he mooched around until the bell was sounded for 'end of lunch break' and he completely blanked her out as he queued to get back into the classroom. Emma certainly noticed the off-hand way in which he ignored her every attempt to get his attention, and she was beginning to get a bit worried. Every time she approached him he turned his back on her and pretended to be interested in what the nearest group of boys were babbling about.

Later that day he picked up his 'A' Level results from the school gymnasium and squashed the envelope into his pocket. Tomorrow is the last day of term, but Art's heart was heavy in the knowledge that he may never see Emma again.

He didn't wait for Emma at the gates at school chucking out time. He just continued his purposeful stride down the road.

When he got home he dashed upstairs three at a time and grabbed the envelope from his pocket. Sitting on the edge of the bed he impatiently tore open the envelope and read its contents.

Mum appeared at the doorway. "Well?" she asked. "What's the news?"

It took the news some time to sink in - all of about two minutes. Art looked up at Mum with a look of astonishment on his face.

"Aced every exam!" he declared.

"Well done. I knew you could do it," she lied. Sitting on the bed next to Art she gave him a hug and kissed his cheek. He wiped the kiss off with his sleeve and smiled at Mum's proud face. This was just the lift that Art needed, thanks to Entity.

The following day, Wednesday, he took the letter in to show teacher and anyone else who never believed he could do so well. Even Emma and the crowd were privileged enough to see the results. Most of that day was taken up with the sixth form spending the time comparing their results and busily chatting between themselves, and to teachers, about what their next move would be. The pupils were counselled about which Uni to go to, if they didn't already have one in mind, and everyone finished the day in a happy and boisterous mood.

Art made his way out of the school gates at going home time and felt more up-beat about going home alone. Three or four minutes into his journey he felt the back of his blazer being tugged. Turning to see who was trying to get his attention he faced Emma. She put on a half-smile, still worried that Art might blank her out. They both stood there, trying to think of something to say, when they suddenly spoke in unison.

"Congrats on your results," they both blurted out at the same time.

Bursting into laughter, all the hurt of Monday and Tuesday that they both had suffered seemed to be forgotten. They hugged each other for a long time and when they eventually parted from the hug Art saw that Emma was crying.

"What's wrong?" giving her his well-used hanky.

After blowing her nose then wiping the tears from her cheeks she said "I'm sorry we were so rotten to you on Monday." She waited for a response, but got none, so she continued, "All the girls in the class had to go to the assembly hall to be lectured about not having sex until we were married. That's why I was late. I just came out with the crowd. I wasn't with them intentionally. We were just coming out together, that's all."

Art realised what a prat he had been.

"I'm sorry as well. When you hooked onto my arm I thought you wanted me to join the crowd. I shouldn't have stormed off like that."

"No, I didn't want that. I just did what I did every time you and Billy waited for me at the gates."

"Yeah ... Billy," misery in his voice at the mention of Billy's name.

"What? What do you mean?"

"I was going to ask you to the pictures, but you and the crowd just made fun of me."

"No, Art. You've got it all wrong. On the way up the drive to the gates I told the crowd that I was going to ask *you* out! They were all disappointed that they hadn't asked you first."

"What, me?"

"Yes, you!"

"I ... I ... What about Billy? Aren't you and he…"

"Billy? Billy is an idiot. Everybody at school thinks he's a prat. He thinks he's God's gift but he's a nobody."

"But I thought all the girls fancied him."

"No, they don't. They only act that way to make him *think* they fancy him. They're taking the piss."

"Uhh? What about Denise, and Janice? He told Mike and me that they had done it with him."

"They went out with him once, and they got so fed up trying to keep his hands off them that they walked out on him."

"But the crowd all huddle together and grin and have secret whispers every time I walk past them. I thought they were having a laugh at my expense."

"You idiot. They were whispering about how much *they* fancied *you*, and how much they wanted to get *you* into the back row of the pictures."

Art stood there, aghast. Why didn't the girls say something to him…? He'd forgotten how shy he was at opening up about such things.

Emma continued, "Do you still want to go to the pictures?"

"Er… Yeah, do I!" Art nodding his head furiously, his eyes wide in surprise.

"Tomorrow?"

"Yeah"

Emma moved closer to Art, gently hooked her arms around his waist and pulled Art to her. After a long look into each other's eyes, she kissed him. A long and loving kiss...

*

On the Friday after the Thursday that Emma and Art sat in the back row of the pictures Art's mum told him that Billy's mum had told her that Billy was okay to have visitors 'cos he was no longer infectious.

"I'll go round today," he confirmed.

He went to Billy's house after seeing Emma home and giving her a lasting kiss goodbye for the night. They agreed to meet up tomorrow, Saturday, to hang out together and go to the cinema.

Art's visit to Billy's house didn't turn out to be quite as friendly as Art had really wanted. He told Billy that he and Emma were now a couple and he had to leave Billy's house with Billy shouting profanities at him as he left the bedroom. It appeared that Billy was annoyed at Art for making a move on Emma in his absence.

'*Too bad*,' thought Art. '*If only Billy knew what the rest of the class thought of him…*'

*

Art's good luck lasted for many years.

He and Emma went to the same University and they both helped each other get through the course. They were inseparable.

Art went on to become a doctor, then a brain surgeon. Emma also became a doctor and she was given a good position in a government research laboratory until she left employment to bring up her two children.

Life couldn't be better for them both and they both always had fond memories of the time they were school kids.

Entity was proud of his handywork…

CHAPTER 8

June Gracey and Sister Gracey June

Sister Gracey, previously Miss Gracey June, lives an idyllic life of a catholic nun in a convent in a beautiful, scenic valley in France. The convent is associated with a monastery about two miles away where ten catholic monks live, work and pray. The monks manage a vineyard surrounding the monastery, from which a world famous wine is produced. The income from this vineyard fully supports the convent and the monastery, so the nuns and monks don't need to go out begging.

Following a probationary period of about 12 months, the nuns in this particular convent attend a ceremony to become 'married' to God. An Ordination ceremony. At this time they vow to remain celibate. Once a virgin, always a virgin… Maybe. That's the rule, anyway.

The nuns are allowed to have computers and modern swipe-style mobile phones, but their vows forbid them to play computer games or bet online - or anywhere else if it comes to that.

They all rise at four a.m. to attend prayers, have breakfast and prepare themselves for their work. So what work do they do? Well, their working days are long and varied. Some are designated to be 'gardeners', tending the vegetable gardens that surround the convent, some are designated to be 'housekeepers', managing and cleaning the convent and cooking meals.

Several of them are designated to attend to the monks; managing and cleaning the monastery, cooking the monks' meals, cleaning and mending their robes and even running their baths when asked. After all, the monks are really busy with their praying and wine pressing and, of course, their flagellation. The attending nuns also dress the monks' wounds after flagellation.

The nuns count themselves extremely lucky to have been given the 'calling' to service. Their hard work is rewarded with a roof over their heads, a bed for the night, free meals, free uniforms, companionship, and the freedom to go to town whenever they wish, subject to them honouring their vows.

Gracey June became a nun several years ago. She didn't tell anyone in the order that she wasn't a virgin when she went for her interview. Nobody ever asked. They just *assumed* that she was a virgin. Losing her virginity was something all the girls in her class did once they reached the age of sixteen, so it was nothing special, at the time. It was just a teenage fad. A trend. Something that had to be done to remain part of the crowd.

Nonetheless, Sister Gracey, as she is now known, never forgot the fun times she had while learning not to be a virgin.

*

June Gracey was a typically angry teenager. Absolutely everything that was wrong in the world was all her dad's fault.

She was unlucky with boyfriends. Here's just one example why; her dad had had the misfortune to be seen, by her, downtown one day while she and a boy from school were bunking off classes to enjoy a Nando's, which the boy had paid for. Dad didn't actually see the pair in Nando's, but that didn't matter. The fact is, the boy didn't take a liking to June so he ditched her, so she blamed Dad just for being there. "He saw you!" was her reason for blaming Dad. That particular incident, she would argue, was the reason she never had a boyfriend, but the real reason was more to do with her own lifestyle and attitude.

She was clumsy and constantly broke things. She would tear her favourite jeans pocket on a door handle. Her hair would never do what she wanted it to do and, much to her embarrassment, her boobs didn't develop into the enviable size that her friends' boobs had. Not one boy had ever asked for a grope, or even came close to making an unrequested grab. All the above, and more, was her dad's fault. At least that was her excuse, at the time, for having so much bad luck.

Her bad luck dogged her into her grown-up life. She obtained average marks at university so finished with an average degree - Dad's fault. She missed the bus that should have taken her to her first interview and so was late. She didn't get the job she really wanted because of her lateness. Again Dad's fault.

And so the catalogue of misfortunes continued, day after day, even into her married life.

She didn't marry the bloke she really wanted to marry because she never met that particular bloke. The bloke that eventually asked her to marry him was, in her books, a 'desperation' husband because her knight in shining armour had just not shown himself and it would soon be too late to have children. A bad mistake based on poor judgement on her part.

What about children? Well, she had one child. A girl. Remembering the painful way in which she grew up she really wanted a boy but, as luck would have it, she was now faced with the daughter from Hell, in much the same way that June's dad had labelled June!

Truth is, her life's ups and downs had been steered by Entity in much the same way that Entity had guided Sister Gracey's life, and right now June Gracey's bad luck quota is seventy-five percent depleted, while Sister Gracey has just twenty-five percent of her good luck quota remaining.

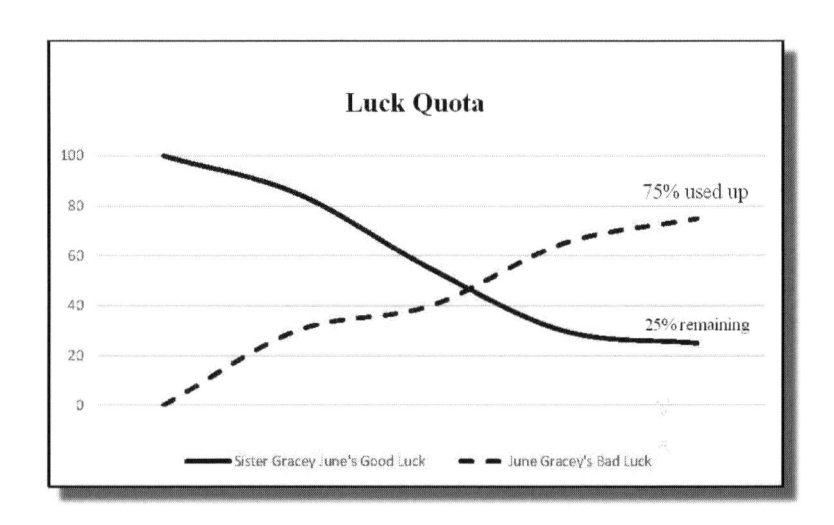

Luck Quota

- Sister Gracey June's Good Luck: 25% remaining
- June Gracey's Bad Luck: 75% used up

Read on to see how these two women's luck changes.

CHAPTER 9

Sister Gracey June's Luck

Let me remind you about Nuns. The nuns are allowed to have computers and telephones, but their vows forbid them to play computer games or bet online. At ordination they are supposed to be virgins, and once married to God they are supposed to remain virgins.

Sister Gracey's sheltered life is about to be turned upside down. Her remaining twenty-five percent of good luck is rapidly running out.

She is one of the chosen few nuns to be housekeeper for one of the monks. Although this means that she has a two mile walk to work, she considers herself lucky that she wasn't instructed by Mother Superior to work in the kitchen, washing the pots and pans and crockery after meal times. There are lots of pots and pans to scrub clean and there is a huge pile of mealtime crockery to wash, dry and put away until the next round of scrubbing. This job is, in fact, Mother Superior's 'punishment' duty for straying too far from one's vows.

Mother Superior is quite tolerant as far as the nun's vows are concerned. She knows that the occasional blasphemous swear word sometimes slips from the nun's mouth. For example, if a gardener's finger is pricked by a rose bush, or a housekeeper drops a bowl of water. She has even heard a nun's vocabulary slip when a few drops of red wine drip from the jug while she is pouring and she, herself, has been known to utter the occasional expletive. After all, accidents happen and Mother Superior is well aware that people just cannot go through life without getting frustrated sometimes. So she lets these minor gaffes go unpunished unless, of course, the gaffe is more than a minor slip of the tongue.

In Sister Gracey's case, however, her gaffes are much, much more than minor!

Now, nuns are not supposed to have any vices whatsoever. Not having any vices is one of the nun's vows. They are supposed to be lily white. Ultra innocent. Let's face it, though, everyone has at least one vice, don't they? Some nuns are known to sneak out through the kitchen door and hide somewhere to have a crafty puff on a cigarette. Mother Superior is aware of this, but she keeps quiet about it until she catches one of them. After all, nothing can be proved, can it? But if a nun is caught by Mother Superior having a sneaky cigarette the ranks of the pan scrubbers is expanded by one.

One of Sister Gracey's vices is playing on-line games. Such a transgression is definitely frowned upon. In the convent, computer games are banned for life. Never to be seen or even spoken of. It's a hard job keeping Sister Gracey's vice secret. She always waits until 'lights out' time to get under her bed covers, turn on her phone and tap the app that opens her game. She has followed this routine for some time now, and the game keeps her attention held long into the early hours. She has become addicted to the game but even though she has to rise from her bed at four a.m., she sometimes plays until three-thirty.

Apart from the fact that she is extremely whacked-out during the day, Entity has noticed how lucky she has been in not getting caught. Mother Superior often asks if Sister Gracey is okay but Gracey just smiles and replies "I'm okay." Each and every time she goes on-line to play her game her quota of good luck is reduced by one percent. She is now down to eight percent remaining. It will soon be time for Entity to reset her life's luck quota.

One afternoon, after Sister Gracey had returned from the monastery having completed all her work there, she was called to Mother Superior's office. Nervously, she made her way down the corridors of the convent humming to the angelic sound of the convent choir. Had she been found out about her on-line gaming? Had one of the other nuns turned her in? How could that be? Surely, no-one knows what she does after 'lights out'?

Arriving at Mother Superior's office she lightly taps on the door and waits for the call to "Enter."

"Good afternoon Sister Gracey. Please, take a seat." Mother Superior points to the wicker chair in front of her desk.

"I know you have finished your duties at the monastery, but I must ask you to go there again. Immediately."

"Oh? why is that? Is there a problem with my work?" Has Brother Gilbert complained?"

"No, of course not. Brother Gilbert has reported nothing but good comments about you, Sister Gracey. He adores you. No, he hasn't complained but he does require an urgent visit. He was found weak and unable to walk after you had departed from the monastery, and the Abbot thinks he may have overdone his flagellation somewhat. His clothes and bedding are covered in blood and his injuries need tending to. Will you go there with haste?"

"Of course I will. I'll gather some bandages and take cleansing ointment with me. I do hope he will be all right."

"God will watch over him, I'm sure. Off you go and please, keep me informed of his progress."

Sister Gracey left Mother Superior's office, gathered her medical bag under her arm and made her way to the monastery. On arrival, the Abbot quickly ushered her to Brother Gilbert's cell.

The scene before her shocked Sister Gracey. Brother Gilbert was sat on his bed, staring at the floor. When Gracey entered the cell he looked up and smiled at her.

"Hello, Sister Gracey. I'm sorry you have to see me in this state."

"Hush now, Brother Gilbert. I'll have you cleaned up in no time." She turned to face the Abbot. "Is there anywhere private we can go while I clean him up? I'll also need his room to be empty for cleaning, as well."

"Of course," replied the Abbot, "The adjacent room is free. I'll arrange for him to be taken there immediately so that you can tend to his wounds. Please, let me know when you need some help getting Brother Gilbert back to his room." the Abbot prompted.

When Brother Gilbert had been helped to the adjacent cell by the Abbot and Brother François, Sister Gracey set about cleaning up his cell and re-making his bed with crisp, clean sheets. She then went next door to help him back to his own cell.

As Gracey helped Gilbert down the corridor, her arm around his waist, she couldn't help feeling his roving hand straying onto her bottom.

Back in Gilbert's cell, Gracey helped him out of his habit and sat him in his bedside chair. It was the first time she had seen him 'in the flesh', so to speak, and she couldn't help thinking what a handsome body the monk had. He had clearly taken extremely good care of his physique, with its six-pack stomach and bulging biceps. Her memories of the fun she had losing her virginity came flooding back to her and she found it extremely difficult tending to Gilbert's injuries with her shaking hands.

"You have a gentle touch," enthused Gilbert. Gracey blushed. By the time Sister Gracey had finished tending to Gilbert's injuries he had recovered from his dizzy spell. He had quaffed several beakers of ale and he was now feeling better… Much better!

Helping him to his feet, she turned to face Gilbert so as to ease him down onto the side of his bed. His roving hand sneakily eluded gravity to float upwards and plant itself firmly on Gracey's boob. It was now blatantly clear what Brother Gilbert's thoughts, and wishes, were as he gently massaged Gracey's boob with closed eyes and a smile on his face that yelled 'Sheer ecstasy!'

Decision time… Should Gracey obey her vow of celibacy and walk away, or should she trust to luck that nobody would disturb them and give in to the sins of the flesh?

There was no competition. Gracey's memories were just too much to ignore and she stood in front of Gilbert with the same 'Sheer ecstasy!' smile on her face. They both knew where this was going, and she hurriedly disrobed and lay on the bed with Gilbert.

*

Now, Entity had been watching Sister Gracey's good luck quota slowly diminish, and with just zero point one percent of good luck remaining, Entity waited with baited breath to see when her good luck would finally run out. It didn't…

*

The Abbot sat in his office cogitating about Brother Gilbert's over enthusiastic flagellation. Wondering if he should speak to Gilbert about it his reflections were brought to a sudden halt. With a start he suddenly wondered how Sister Gracey was getting on with cleaning up Brother Gilbert and his cell. It had been some time now since he had left her tending to Gilbert's injuries but he hadn't heard anything from her. Perhaps he should amble down to the cell to see if she was anywhere near finished.

Gracey was nowhere near finished when the Abbot poked his head round Gilbert's cell door to see them both in the midst of their fornication. He coughed, loudly, to attract attention. His cough worked. The two fornicators suddenly stopped what they were doing and Gilbert got off the top of Gracey. Gracey tried to cover her body with some bedclothes, but wasn't very successful. She covered her face instead.

After a long pause, while Gilbert gathered up his habit in front of himself, the Abbot sternly ordered, " Brother Gilbert, I'll see you in my office when you have finished dressing. Sister Gracey, leave the monastery and do not return. I will be sending a full report of this liaison to Mother Superior."

The Abbot disappeared into the corridor and Gracey and Gilbert listened to his footsteps fading away. They looked at each other, smiled, nodded and then returned to finish what they had started.

However, Gracey's good luck quota was now fully depleted. It was time for Entity to reset Gracey's life quota of luck.

On her return to the convent Gracey was, once more, called to Mother Superior's office.

"Would you like to offer an explanation of what went on with Brother Gilbert?"

Gracey was silent. Her face was sullen but inwardly she was smiling that 'Sheer ecstasy!' smile.

Hearing no response, Mother Superior declared, "I'll take that as a no, then. What are we to do with you, Sister Gracey?"

Gracey was tempted to say "Nothing," but thought better of it. Silence is golden in a situation such as this.

"I'm loath to defrock you, Gracey. You do too much good work here and in the community, but your sin cannot go unpunished. What do you suggest would be a good punishment?"

"Relegated to the kitchen to scrub the pots and wash the crockery?"

"All right, Sister Gracey. That is what you will do. But heed my warning! If you are caught transgressing your vows again I will have no alternative but to send you out of this convent to fend for yourself in the world outside."

"Thank you Reverend Mother," was all that Gracey replied before leaving Mother Superior's office to draw out an apron and take some other nun's place in the kitchen… With that secret 'Sheer ecstasy!' smile still in her minds eye.

CHAPTER 10

June Gracey's Luck

What can I tell you about June Gracey's luck that I haven't already told you?

Well, we know that she married some bloke that she didn't really want to marry. Her husband turned out to be a proper waster. Now that was just bad luck in itself but, to cap it all, the guy was caught dipping into his firm's accounts without permission and he went on the run to avoid some jail time. He's never been seen since. This, in effect, increased June's bad luck depletion to ninety percent. Her life's luck quota was close to being reset, but it was not quite close enough, yet.

Just before her husband disappeared June went and got pregnant by him once more. Guess what? She had another girl. Now that was bad luck, to say the least. Just when her first daughter was settling down a second daughter from hell appeared! Battle on, June. You've been through it before so you know how to handle bad mannered, grumpy daughters.

June's bad luck quota is now ninety-five percent depleted.

Because her husband was no longer around June found it necessary to take on some jobs to pay the bills. She tried the local job centre, but part time jobs were few and far between. Then a neighbour asked her to clean her (the neighbour's) home while she went out to do her office job somewhere in the city. News travelled fast and another neighbour, then another, joined in and June found herself going to three homes each week to clean them, make the beds, wash up all the breakfast stuff, load the washing machine, empty the washing machine, do the ironing and take out the bins. It was hard work and a miserable existence, but the money saw her through her eldest daughter's university accommodation costs together with her own household bills. She took her youngest daughter with her to each of the houses she was cleaning.

With her elder daughter now at university and her younger daughter still in nappies, June had time to kill on the days that she wasn't house cleaning. She filled her time by playing an on-line game. She got quite good at it, actually, despite her quota of bad luck sometimes getting in the way.

However, her five percent of bad luck waiting to be fully depleted reared its ugly head one morning while she was cleaning a neighbour's house. This happened on a Friday morning. The neighbour had informed June that she, and her family, were going away for the weekend and wouldn't be back until Tuesday, but June can let herself in to do the cleaning. June realised that cleaning the house on this particular Friday was a gift because she wouldn't need to return on the following Monday to clean again because the house had not been used over the weekend. A day of free money because she would still be paid for Monday's non-visit. If she did a good job on the Friday, the neighbour would never know that she didn't come in on Monday.

June left daughter number two downstairs on the lounge floor while she went upstairs to make the beds. Now, you know what young children are like, don't you? They get into everything. They open cupboards and rake out the cupboard's contents. They pull cushions off the furniture and throw them everywhere. They yank on any electric flex that happens to be hanging loose and they have a predilection for pushing any button they can reach.

While June was upstairs the kid wrecked the room. Table lamps got pulled off the tables, cushions got thrown everywhere - and sat on while the girl had a wee that escaped out of her nappy. Snot was snuffled over the furniture, sick was sicked onto the carpet, ornaments were knocked off the shelves by the flying cushions, buttons were pushed on every reachable gadget that had a button that could be pushed, and DVD's from a cupboard were strewn everywhere. An upturned lamp had been switched on and the exposed bulb had burnt through its flimsy shade and charred the settee cushion.

June stopped what she was doing upstairs when she heard the television shouting to the neighbourhood with hundreds of decibels. Dashing downstairs to see what the din was about she was horrified to see her daughter happily banging the TV remote control on the floor, the way that kids bang stuff on the floor to get it to do something. June surveyed the wrecked room in horror, realising that she should have taken her daughter upstairs when she went to make the beds instead of leaving her on her own, in the lounge, to create havoc.

Cursing the child loudly, she set about clearing up the mess, after firstly strapping the child into the push chair to stop her getting in the way. It took an extra two hours of hard labour to clean the place up. Cushion covers had to be washed, dried and ironed before being replaced, carpet had to be scrubbed clean of sick, ornaments had to be put back - those that were not broken, anyway - table lamps had to be replaced and DVD's had to be wiped clean of snot, returned to their cases and put back into the cupboard.

When June had finished, she scanned the room for anything else that might indicate that a wrecking ball had smashed its way through the lounge. Satisfied that things *looked* normal she left the house to return home to feed the wrecking ball.

On Tuesday evening June's front doorbell chimed. June tutted as she went to answer the door. She was just at an important juncture in her on-line game and didn't want to pause it.

Answering the door she was faced with her neighbour. Inviting the neighbour in, she went to the kitchen to make a pot of tea and returned to her lounge. The neighbour kicked off straight away.

"What happened to my lounge while we were away?" she asked, pointedly.

"Er, what do you mean?" replied June.

"Something happened while we were away!" the neighbour hissed.

"What? I don't know what you mean?"

"Yes, you do. Some of my ornaments were broken. I found the pieces in the bin this morning."

"Oh, yes. I'm sorry, I had an accident."

"An accident? Why didn't you tell me about the burn mark on the settee, and why were all the DVD's in the wrong case, in the wrong order in the wrong cupboard?"

"Yes, well…" June knew she had been rumbled and she tried to explain. "I left my daughter in the lounge while I made the beds. I forgot to strap her in the push chair before I went upstairs and…"

She was abruptly interrupted. "Do you realise what your brat has done?" the neighbour spat.

"Well, I tried to clean up after her, to put things right. I'll replace the ornaments…"

She was interrupted again. "The TV box has been turned off. Absolutely NOTHING has been recorded over the weekend. My husband is furious. He missed the football match."

"I'm so sorry," pleaded June, "Please give him my apologies. It won't happen again."

"You're damned right it won't happen, June, because I don't want you in my house again."

The neighbour stormed out of June's house leaving her tea to go cold.

'*What rotten luck!*' thought June. '*If only I had thought to take the kid upstairs with me.*'

June's rotten luck didn't end there.

Several weeks after the event June received a letter from her neighbour threatening legal action if June didn't buy a new three-piece suite to replace the burnt settee, together with a demand for an extra two hundred pounds to replace the broken ornaments. June didn't have two hundred pence, let alone two hundred pounds… Plus the cost of a new three-piece suite.

Now that's what you call bad luck, but Entity had heard the alarm bell shouting out from its system and June's life's luck quota was reset immediately. It was about time June had some good luck.

*

At first, June didn't know her life's luck quota had been reset.

She carried on with her mundane life, cleaning her two neighbours' homes for them, washing her daughter's snot ridden clothes - and hair - and enjoying her free time with the on-line game. The two neighbours had heard about

June's disaster but both, fortunately, took pity on her and decided to keep her on as their cleaner.

Then one morning she received two official looking envelopes. The return address on one was from a solicitor in the city. She knew what that one was about because she had not yet provided her neighbour with any reparations for the damage caused at the neighbour's house. The other envelope was a mystery. It was a plain brown envelope with absolutely no indication of where it was from. June opened this envelope first.

Inside was a letter from the premium bond people informing her that she had won a major prize and that she should contact the number shown as soon as possible to claim it. June's heart skipped a beat. *'Maybe there will be enough to pay back the neighbour?'* she thought. *'That would be nice. I'll phone later.'*

Yep, the other letter was from the neighbour's solicitor demanding a sum of three thousand, six hundred pounds; two thousand, six hundred pounds for a new three-piece suite, six hundred pounds for broken ornaments, three hundred pounds for re-cleaning of carpets and cushion covers and a further one hundred pound for loss of TV services while the box was switched off. There was also a demand for an immediate payment of one thousand five-hundred pounds for redecorating the lounge because the neighbour thought she noticed a snot stain on one of the walls.

June sat down and cried for a while. Five thousand, one hundred pounds! There was no way she had that kind of money, and with the best will in the world it would take years to pay back… With interest. She reflected on how heartless her neighbour was.

Then she remembered her other letter. The premium bond win. '*With my luck, it will be just a few quid,*' she thought. Drying her eyes and taking a deep breath she dialled the number on the letter.

The phone was answered almost immediately. The woman on the other end of the line introduced herself and asked how she could help.

"I've received a letter from you telling me that I've won a prize."

"Congratulations, Mrs Gracey. Can I just ask you some security questions?"

"Of course."

Security questions done, the woman from the premium bond people then went on to let June know what prize she had won.

"It gives me great pleasure, Mrs. Gracey, to inform you that you have won this week's top prize of **one million pounds**…!"

Entity stabbed his re-set button…

There was a long pause while June let the words sink in.

"Are you still there, Mrs. Gracey? Are you okay?"

"Oh, yes. I'm fine, thank you What… What… What happens next?"

The premium bond woman went through the procedure of how to claim the prize and June took copious notes. Thanking the premium bond woman she replaced the telephone receiver, sat back and once more cried, only this time the tears were tears of joy, not despair.

*

June managed to pay off her debt to her neighbour. She didn't let on to anyone where she got the money from or that she had come up big on the premium bond. That would be her secret…

CHAPTER 11

Enzo Lorenzo & Lorenzo Enzo

Enzo (Eni) Lorenzo and Lorenzo (Lory) Enzo have never met face-to-face, although they do know of each other. It's unlikely that they'll ever meet in person because Eni lives in Spain and Lory lives in Italy, but... You never know.

They are both chefs, and they both own restaurant businesses. They are both famous and they both enjoy lots of TV airtime in their respective countries. They have both been introduced to famous celebrities, sometimes to the same celebrity but on a different day, on a different TV channel and at a different time, and their restaurants enjoy patronage from several famous dignitaries. Sometimes a dignitary makes a secret visit with a secret guest before going on to a little known secret hotel, but everyone knows how discreet the chefs and their staff are. That's why the dignitaries and famous celebrities use Eni's and Lory's restaurants.

Newspaper reporters are not welcome. Nor are they ever invited.

Entity has been watching Eni and Lory. It knows that Eni's quota of good luck is about to run out and that Lory's quota of bad luck will shortly tip the scales of luck in his favour, but it is not yet time for any of this to happen.

Eni's Good Luck	Lory's Bad Luck
	30%
	30%
10%	30%

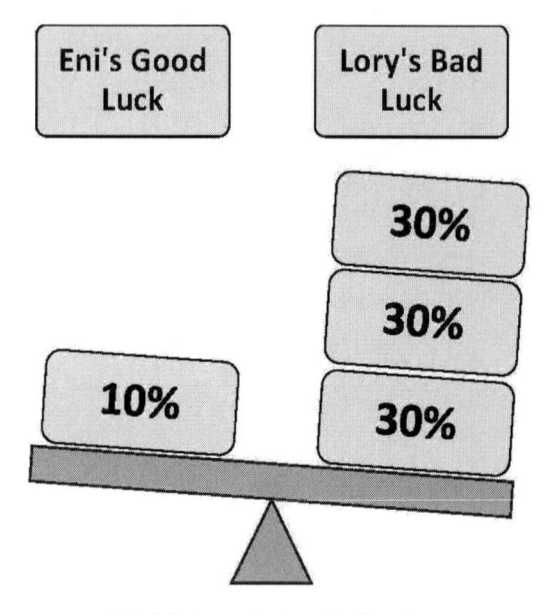

Eni & Lory's Luck Quota

The chefs communicate with each other regularly on their social media pages. They chat, they swap recipes and they swap stories about how their restaurants are doing - who has recently visited, what they had to eat, who they met - that kind of thing. During one of their internet meetings Lory related how he was in the middle of a run of bad luck. We'll hear about the bad luck he's experienced and, indeed, what bad luck he will suffer, in a moment.

    Eni was pleased with his life. His restaurant is perpetually busy with lots of meals to prepare, and serve, to a long list of celebrities. His clientele of famous dignitaries has recently increased to include several politicians, some of them occasionally bringing a 'friend' wearing a low-cut dress and lots of charisma - a 'friend' who is not their wife…

*

Entity can multi-task. One finger hovers over Eni's life's luck reset button while the finger on his other hand hovers over Lory's life's luck reset button. Any moment now Entity will stab both buttons at once to reset the life luck of the chefs. All it is waiting for is that alarm to sound, and it will breathe a sigh of satisfaction to mark a job well done, but it is impatient and would greatly like to speed up the life luck re-setting process.

The alarm never sounded! It never had the chance to go off because Lory threw a curved ball at Entity's plan. A curve so bent that it locked Entity out of Eni and Lory's database of luck quota, similar to the way your computer at home sometimes locks you out… But this lock is so tight Entity will not get access to their quota of life luck, for quite some time.

So what happened?

CHAPTER 12

Enzo (Eni) Lorenzo's Luck

I'm going to start by telling you all about Eni's luck.

As a world renowned chef, Eni has enjoyed lots of praise for his culinary skills, his recipe books, his menus, his presentation talents, his hosting proficiencies and, above all else, his discretion. Eni didn't get where he is today by being indiscreet, a well versed fact that he repeatedly sprouts to his workforce.

It is also a well-known fact that Eni will not, under any circumstances, allow a TV or newspaper reporter anywhere near his restaurant's front door. He loathes them. They annoy his famous and most valued clientele, they disrupt meals with their intrusive behaviour – sticking microphones in the face of their victims and demanding answers to interfering and unpleasant questions – and they all expect freebies when they come banging on the restaurant door to try to get permission to enter. Eni's social media pages are littered with many uncomplimentary comments about his refusal to entertain TV or newspaper reporters, but such comments just go to increase his loathing of them.

Out of necessity he accepts invitations for TV appearances, but his actions belie his silky smooth demeanour in front of the cameras. Any suggestion of an irritating question and he's on his feet, on a path to the stage door and on his way out of the studio. TV interviewers know this.

They've all had this treatment so they try to steer clear of such irritation. They treat Eni with utter respect, but their respect is rarely reciprocated. Eni didn't get where he is today by respecting reporters and TV interviewers - another of his well versed maxims.

I've mentioned Eni's social media pages. This is where he and Lory enjoy each other's company. They swap recipes and tell each other about their clientele, sometimes just 'passing the time of day'. They are both, however, very discreet about what they say on social media. They never say a bad thing about their clients, or about each other.

They have promised to visit each other's restaurant, some time, to taste the other's culinary delights but neither of them has ever found the time to take that leap.

Now, there is a saying that epitomises the human race. It goes, 'The more people I meet, the more I like my dog.' This maxim has been around for a while and there's a lot of candour attached to it.

*

One morning, Eni got a telephone call from a notable dignitary. A VIP. A famous politician.

"Enzo, my friend, have you got a spare table for two for tonight?"

"For you, Pablo, always."

"Excellent. Usual time?"

"No problem."

Pablo arrived, as discussed, and he and his 'guest' were shown to his favourite discreet corner table by the waitress. Table nine. His guest was another notable luminary. A VIP. Another famous female politician wearing a [very] low cut, see-through Versace dress that could only be described as a wide belt... Not Pablo's wife.

On the way to his table Pablo surreptitiously fondled the waitress's buttock. Now, all of Eni's staff are vetted and trained to the highest standards. Naturally, their training dedicated a large amount of time to the subject of 'discretion.' Being ultra-discreet, the waitress didn't make any fuss about Pablo's roving hand, she just carried on as if nothing had happened.

But the roving hand had not gone unnoticed by Eni. He, too, remained discreet... For the time being.

As the evening progressed it became clear that the intentions of the occupants at table nine were far from honourable. There was much billing and cooing, supplemented with copious glasses of the best wine, constant holding hands and frequent face stroking. Pablo was extremely lucky to have persuaded his guest to spend the night with him. She was due to fly off to a sunny climate tomorrow afternoon for some topless sun worshipping. She would be away for about a fortnight so there was no doubt that the pair will, at some stage tonight, occupy a discreet corner room in a discreet corner hotel on a discreet street corner somewhere close by to bolster their friendship. That was none of Eni's business. He was there to provide a five-star meal, provide five-star service, be discreet and respect his client's privacy.

Eni's good luck quota was now only about five percent available! He really should start to look for ways to improve this.

Towards the latter part of the meal the silence of the dining area was disrupted by shouting between the two people seated at table nine. Maybe the wine had got to them. Maybe Pablo had said, or done, something that offended his guest. Only they knew why their intimate discussion had exploded into an argument, but the woman stood and issued a mighty slap across Pablo's face. She then poured a full glass of wine over his head, pushed over the wine carafe, spilling the liquid over his shirt and trousers, and stormed out of the restaurant. Pablo sat there trying to dry his hair, his shirt and his trousers with a napkin. Oh dear… His night of passionate love-making with his guest was now definitely off the books… Perhaps the waitress could be persuaded to accompany him to his discreet corner room in a discreet corner hotel on a discreet street corner somewhere close by?

Eni was in the kitchen berating his sous chef about something when the fracas occurred. He poked his head out of the kitchen door but was waved back inside by the waitress. She is experienced in this type of thing and could competently handle the matter.

She approached table nine with an armful of napkins and a clean table cloth with the intention of re-laying the wine soaked table for Pablo. Not one to miss an opportunity, he ran his hand up the waitress's skirt on the inside of her thigh. She pushed his hand away brusquely and stepped back. Pablo sat there, smiling. When the waitress continued to re-lay the table Pablo reached up and fondled the woman's breast. She again brushed his hand away. Dumping the pile of napkins and clean tablecloth on the guy's lap she turned her back on him and walked away from the table.

Despite being waved back into the kitchen, Eni had stood with his body half out of the kitchen door watching the drunken antics of the politician. When he saw Pablo grab the waitress's breast, enough was enough. Discretion is one thing, but respect for his staff is demanded by Eni. He casually walked over to table nine, informed Pablo what he had just witnessed and then asked the politician to leave the restaurant. Pablo was, after all, "… disturbing my other clients."

The room was shrouded in a deathly silence as Eni's other clients looked on, waiting for something to happen.

Pablo didn't take kindly to this embarrassing eviction and he threatened all sorts of recriminations. These words didn't cut it with Eni who insisted the guy left the restaurant. He did, however, inform Pablo that he would not be charging him for the meal.

Pablo stood up, threw his napkin down and stormed out of the building. The fresh air must have done something to his digestion because he bent over and vomited his meal onto the pavement in front of the restaurant window.

Okay, this type of incident occurs in almost every restaurant, and the offenders always leave their calling card spread out on the pavement in front of the establishment, don't they? So how do you think this particular incident affected Eni's luck quota?

A member of the paparazzi had been stalking the politician. He had taken several photos of Pablo and his guest entering the restaurant, and he took more shots of the politician's guest as she came out, noting that she was alone and had a dark expression of anger on her face. He got a good photo of that.

The photographer knew that his entry to the restaurant was barred, so he hid in a doorway to await the exit of the politician. His target eventually emerged from the restaurant, and as he was bent over, spewing up his meal, the photographer saw a golden opportunity for a photo that will pay well by the media. Several shots later he watched Pablo zigzagging down the street on unstable legs, sometimes wobbling over the kerb into the gutter. More photo's were taken of the politician's drunken meandering trail to look for a taxi, but Pablo never saw the photographer following behind, happily snapping his drunken performance.

The following day the paparazzi's photo's were splashed across the front page of every newspaper in the world, with derisory comments about his illicit liaison with a 'friend' - not his wife - and his drunken antics.

What, you may ask, does this have to do with Eni's good luck quota?

*

Well, Entity had not yet clicked on Eni's life luck quota button to turn his good luck quota into bad luck. His finger still hovered over Eni's good luck button, waiting for Eni's run of good luck to dwindle to zero - he still had a small amount of good luck available to him - but Eni appears to be spiralling into a really serious phase of bad luck... Without any intervention from Entity, whatsoever!

It seemed that Entity had lost control of the situation and it gasped in surprise at this obvious anomaly.

Entity stared at his screen, wondering where all this was going and what it could do to bring the situation back under his control.

*

After being alerted to the news media's coverage of his previous night's antics, the politician immediately held several news conferences to explain his actions. His excuse for the illicit liaison was that it was a business meeting... Of course it was! However, his excuse for spewing up outside the restaurant was that he *might* - he chose his words carefully - he '*might* have got a bit of food poisoning, but he would be surprised if it was, in any way, related to the restaurant...'

Eni was furious. He took immediate damage limitation steps to sue Pablo for defamation and, courtesy of a TV interviewer - with the promise by Eni of a free meal - made an emergency TV appearance from inside the restaurant to deny all allegations of food poisoning.

Too late. His good name, and that of his restaurant, was badly smeared by every social media platform, newspaper, TV channel and, indeed, by word of mouth. His reputation was so badly tarnished that, in no time at all, his regular celebrities and famous dignitaries made a conscious effort not to patronise his establishment. They made it clear that they didn't want to be associated with an establishment that poisons its clients.

Eni was gutted. With no famous clientele visiting the restaurant for meals and to have photo-shoots outside the building, his business gradually spiralled downwards. Eni, and his business, became debt-ridden. He was in a bad way. His staff all resigned because he couldn't pay their salaries, his suppliers stopped supplying, his friends deserted him and, eventually, he had to take a job flipping burgers just to pay the rent on the now empty restaurant.

Eni's good luck quota was on the cusp of tipping over to fully depleted. Almost maxed out with just one percent good luck available to him.

It has been several weeks since Entity realised that it had lost control of the situation and it was still perplexed over the anomaly that caused Eni's luck to spiral out of control while there was still some good luck available to him. Entity had not yet found a fix.

The curved ball is speeding towards Entity, but Entity has taken his eye off it!

CHAPTER 13

Lorenzo (Lory) Enzo's Luck

Lory has had quite a lot of bad luck.

Early in his school years his mum had a notion that he could sing like an angel, so she 'suggested' that he should be a good catholic and sing in the local church choir. She had visions of him being an opera singer. Actually, he wasn't all that bad and he enjoyed his soloist position in the choir until, that is, his voice broke at an early age and the choir master told him he didn't want a bass singer in the choir pews. He was put off opera singing by that remark.

At school he was a good athlete. He broke the school's record for the one hundred metre, two hundred metre and four hundred metre sprints and he was destined to be an international athlete. Unfortunately he got knocked down by a drunk driver and his right knee was badly damaged. Despite several operations he never fully recovered, so his athletic career was well and truly squashed.

In his third school year he tried his hand at technical drawing. The intention, here, was to get proficient at drawing plans so that he could perhaps become an architect. No joy there. He just couldn't grasp the principle of three dimensional drawing.

In his final school year, while he was at home recovering from his accident, he put his hand to cooking the meals for his mum and dad, who both went out to work full time. Cooking was something that piqued his interest and he enjoyed it, so he persuaded mum to get a load of cook books from the library and he read up on everything he could about the science of cooking.

Because of his accident, and the many operations that followed, he didn't spend much of his final school year at school. Instead, he undertook a course of home schooling over the Internet and obtained some good passes at exam time. Enough to get him into cooking college.

The college was not as good as a university, but Lory stuck at it and gained a lot of credibility for his cooking flair and presentation imagination. He excelled at exam time and, for once, his luck held out long enough for him to become a trainee chef. The following years saw him progress and he honed his expertise enough to become a sous chef for some high powered cook in Rome.

Even so, bad luck shadowed his career. There was a fire in his boss's restaurant kitchen. A fire that badly burned Lory's left arm and neck. That didn't put him off, though. After a period of rehabilitation he returned to cooking, this time owning his own small backstreet restaurant purchased with the compensation he received for his injury.

Although he never looked back, he struggled to look forward. One crisis after another dogged his life. Strikes, riots, even a pandemic hindered his journey through his life's trajectory, but he never gave up. He battled on to become the respected chef that he is today. He now owns a large and famous restaurant in a desirable part of Rome, with a staff of three servers and a sous chef, and he enjoys the social media compliments he constantly receives on his various social pages. Notwithstanding his success, he's had to fight his bad luck all the way to this prominence.

One would think that Lory was enjoying a patch of good luck, but the amount of bad luck he had battled with throughout his life had far outweighed any derisory good luck that may have been bestowed upon him. His bad luck quota, however, was now at the ninety-nine percent level and Entity was eagerly waiting to reset his life's luck quota.

Talking of social media, He read about his friend's downfall. Enzo's downfall.

This bothered him immensely. He saw how easily his social media friend had fallen from grace and he worried that the same could happen to him, given his bad luck. He spoke frequently to his friend via the Zoom app and he tried to lift his friend's spirits to encourage him not to lose heart. He gave Eni numerous examples of how he (Lory) had had to battle on with life, and that life isn't always as cruel as it may now seem, but that didn't cut it with Eni. Eni could see no way out of his nightmare. Eni even intimated that he would need to sell his beloved restaurant business to survive life's cruel blow.

Lory chewed over this for days - and nights. What could he do to help his friend? There must be something.

Then an idea came to him! An idea so extreme that he had to seek advice about it. He invited his trusted accountant and his trusted lawyer over for lunch to discuss the pros and cons of his idea, a free five-star meal his trusted advisors couldn't refuse. After discussing his idea with them and being informed that it was a good one, he telephoned his friend to ask... No, demand that his friend opens

Zoom up at seven p.m. that night to discuss something important. Eni was a little puzzled, but with nothing else to do he agreed.

At seven p.m. that evening Lory invited Eni to the chat room.

"Hi Enzo," he opened up with, "how's things?"

With much sadness in his voice, Eni replied, "Not good, my friend. I've just received a letter from my landlord telling me that unless I put the empty restaurant to some use he will need to evict me because he has several lucrative clients queueing up to pay him more rent than I do."

"That's not good news. How are you getting on with your law suit against the politician?"

"That? Oh, that's come to a standstill. I can't get any further with that because I cannot afford my legal fees. Those fees are going to cripple me in any event, even if I win. The politician has even upped the ante by issuing a charge against me for food poisoning him."

"Enzo, I hope you don't mind, but I've discussed your predicament with my advisors and they tell me that all is not lost. Can I tell you what they say?"

"What's the point Lorenzo? There is nothing anyone can do to get me out of this hole. It is the worse time of my life, and I'm thinking of packing it all in. I'll be flipping burgers for the rest of my life to pay off the lawyers and my rent arrears."

"You don't need to do that Eni. I have a proposal that will interest you."

"Yeah? What can you possibly propose that will get me out of all the trouble I'm in? Have you got a couple of million Euros to bail me out? No. You stay well away from me, 'cos I can only bring you more bad luck."

"Enzo, listen to me!" ordered Lory. "Listen to what I have to say and then perhaps you will change your mind about things."

There was a pause while Enzo let his friend's assertion bounce around the inside of his head.

*

Here comes the curved ball, Entity, and there is nothing you can do to prevent its effect… You've been unable to correct the anomaly!

Lory's bad luck quota was now at ninety-nine percent depleted and Eni's good luck quota hovered around the one percent available mark. Let's see what Lory had to offer that would cause the blue screen of death to appear on Entity's PC screen.

*

"Alright, tell me what you want to tell me," sighed Eni. He was ready to accept his fate and he doubted that anything Lory could say would help in any way.

"Okay, Enzo. Now don't interrupt me and don't think I am proposing this because I feel sorry for you. I do feel sorry for you, but that's not the only reason for my proposal."

Another short pause while Lory got his thoughts in order.

"I want you to be my partner," Lory blurted out. He waited for a response. None.

"Did you hear what I've just said?"

"I heard, but you told me not to interrupt you…"

"Okay, you can speak now."

One word only. "Why?"

Lory gathered his thoughts, once more, to answer Eni.

"Because it will be good for us both. I'll have a working partner in Spain and you'll have a working partner in Italy. A match made in heaven!"

"But why, Lory? What do you get out of this but bad debt and a bad name for being associated with a food poisoner?"

"No, Eni. You're missing the point. My lawyer tells me that, even in Spanish law, there is a good case for you against the politician for defamation, libel, injured reputation, loss of earnings, the lot. With the right kind of legal advice you stand a good chance of returning to your restaurant within weeks. My lawyer has even offered to go over to Spain to act on your behalf pro bono. He's good, Enzo. He will win this for you. He'll even smooth things out with your landlord. You'll be able to bail yourself out of debt, you'll get back your good name and reputation, and you won't need to flip burgers ever again."

"You still haven't told me what you get out of this," Enzo probed.

"What I get out of this?" Lory gasped. "Eni, I'm not proposing this for myself, I'm trying to help you climb out of that dark hole you're in. That's what friends are for."

Enzo thought some more, staring down at his desk with his head in his hand.

"You get a Michelin Star partner, you get a satellite restaurant in Spain and you get to share a hell of a lot of my profit," proffered Enzo. He looked up at the screen and waited for Lory to reply.

With a sigh, Lory said, "It's up to you, my friend. I'm only trying to do what's best for us both, and you're right in what you say, but look at it another way… You get the same as I get! A Michelin Star partner, a satellite restaurant in Italy and a share in a hell of a lot of my profit. We'll both be international chefs, offering international menus!"

After some more thought, Eni choked out a reply. "You are a good and loyal friend, Lory." With tears in his eyes he continued, "I accept."

*

There, you have it, Entity.

By accepting Lory's offer of help, Eni's fortunes would be the same as Lory's and their luck, whether good or bad, would be a shared quota.

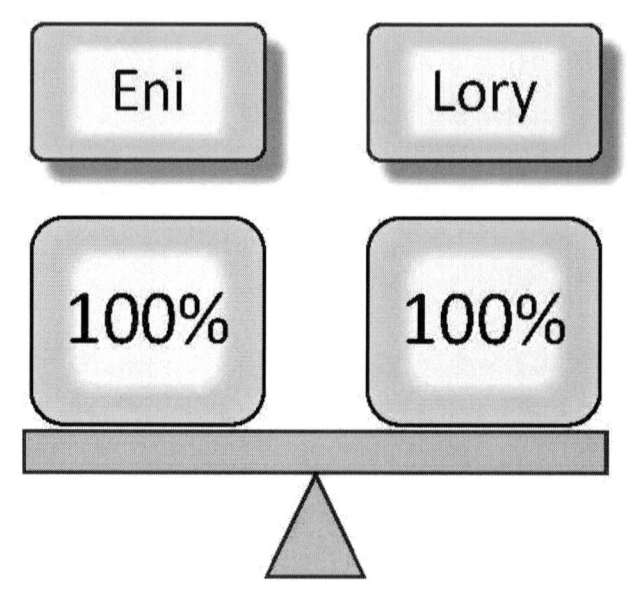

**Eni & Lory's Luck Quota
Re-set by the effects of the curved ball**

Advisors for the two men made several round trips to each other's country to iron out the wrinkles and get the partnership set up.

Lory was correct in his advice regarding the politician. With the help of Lory's lawyer and accountant, Eni received a massive pay-out. Enough not only to bail him out of debt, but with a lot of spare to buy out his landlord to own his restaurant outright, and even some spare to refurbish it to a higher specification.

The partnership lasted until both men died. Even then, the partnership was continued by both men's sons who managed and expanded their restaurants into a thriving international celebrity hub.

*

What of Entity?

It was gobsmacked by Lory's proposal and watched, eyes wide in horror, as the blue screen of death had appeared on all the screens in front of him. The blue screen continued to lock Entity out of Eni's and Lory's life's luck quota system for a long time.

In fact, the blue screen locked Entity out of *everyone's* life luck quota database for a very, very long time…

PART 2

THE GAME

CHAPTER 14

The Gamble

Eight people who, with the exception of two schoolboys, have never met each other face-to-face. Even the two schoolboys had temporarily lost touch with each other since leaving school.

So what is it that connects all eight people at once?

It can only be one thing, can't it? Yep, you've got it… The internet.

There is a multitude of places to meet over the internet; dozens of platforms via social media, gaming apps and chat rooms. And then there is the so called dark web. This is the place where a dark web entity resides.

*

Perhaps now is the time to reveal Entity's real self.

He is the Devil. The Antichrist. Lucifer. Prince of Darkness. Satan. The Fallen Angel. Call him what you will, but he is intent on increasing the size of his flock by using this game, so he disguised it as an innocent on-line game to suck players into his grasp. He is truly evil!

He sat back on his throne to survey all that he commands, his chin resting on his hands resting on his elbows resting on the arms of his throne, and wondered why he had temporarily lost control of the situation with regard to Enzo Lorenzo and Lorenzo Enzo's life's luck quota. One of them had lobbed a curved ball at Entity's system and he finished up with a blue screen staring at him from all his terminals. Puzzling, eh?

Never mind. Entity had re-booted his system after a long and frustrating quest to get it up and running again, and he could now resume control of everyone's life and luck.

He was, however, determined not to lose control of his system again and he kept a constant vigil for any sign of anomalies that could possibly upset his plans for recruitment into his less than privileged, miserable institute.

He tried to keep his eye on the ball, but…

*

Unbeknown to the eight people who have reached the finals in a seemingly innocent internet game, they have all been unwittingly groomed by Entity and they are all now ready to play some serious gaming. What is even more disturbing is that these eight internet gamers are so wrapped up with their game, they don't know that they have been pitted against each other in a sinister way. All they know, at the moment, is that they are playing for a huge prize of four million pounds.

The name of this game? ... It is called 'LUCKY, OR WHAT?'

It is probably time to explain the rules.

There are several rules. In the early stages of the game players must pass certain on-line tests to reach the final eight places.

Rule one:

The first hurdle to leap over is having to pay a sum of one hundred pounds to enter the arena and play the game. Okay, that's not a huge sum for many of us but to some it is a small fortune, especially if you don't have any money or the means to get some in the first place. However, such is the game's popularity it has, so far, netted the game's inventor a vast sum of two hundred million pounds.

Once your entry fee has been accepted your Avatar has lots of lifting, throwing, swinging across ravines, climbing ropes, building bridges and defending itself from a myriad of creatures and other players, all intent on killing you. You have to search for and locate several implements and weapons to defend yourself. In its simplest form the game is, essentially, a knock-out hide and seek competition, each Avatar hiding from a nasty creature - and each other - until they are in a position to reveal their whereabouts to eliminate an opponent.

So, rule two:

Your Avatar can be killed by any creature or any of the other Avatars, but if an Avatar dies along the way that Avatar's owner will lose his entry fee and he is locked out of the game. It has been a long and arduous task but our eight gamers have managed to survive the preliminary rounds to become the eight finalists. None of them realise that what happens to their Avatar in the game, now also happens to them in real life!

This is Entity's twisted way of having fun and increasing his residential club's membership.

Rule three:

All eight finalists are allocated a sum of two hundred and fifty-thousand pounds. They can cash this in now, before going any further, or they can decline to accept this sum and continue with the game to win four million pounds... If they are lucky enough.

Rule four:

If any of the finalists decides to cash in their award and leave the game, the final pot of winnings is reduced by that amount. The more that decide to cash in at this point, the less there will be in the final winnings pot.

So, the finalists now have a decision to make. Do they cash in their award of two hundred and fifty-thousand pounds, or do they gamble this on their ability to win the top prize? Now that's a lot of money and one needs a hell of a lot of luck to stay alive and win the game to take that pot. However, we all know that greed overcomes common sense, don't we?

For an initial outlay of one hundred pounds any one of the eight finalists can, right now, cash in on two-thousand five-hundred times that amount. But every finalist has allowed their greed to get the better of them and all have elected to gamble away their award by continuing with the game. So the winner could boost his bank account by forty-thousand times his initial game entry outlay… If luck is on his side.

Something else the finalists don't realise is that they have been shunted out of an innocent on-line game into the world of the dark web. As far as they are concerned, they are just playing an on-line game of hide and seek.

Avatars have been chosen, contestants have been fed and watered, and everyone has limbered up… So let the game begin.

*

Entity has managed to reset all the finalist's life luck quota and they all now have just ten percent of good luck available to them.

Entity's plan is to make sure that everyone has *nothing* but bad luck. Do you recall what happens to a person who has *nothing* but bad luck?

Eight players. Eight avatars. Remember - if you die, you lose. If you lose, you die…

Either way - you're dead!

ELIMINATION ROUNDS

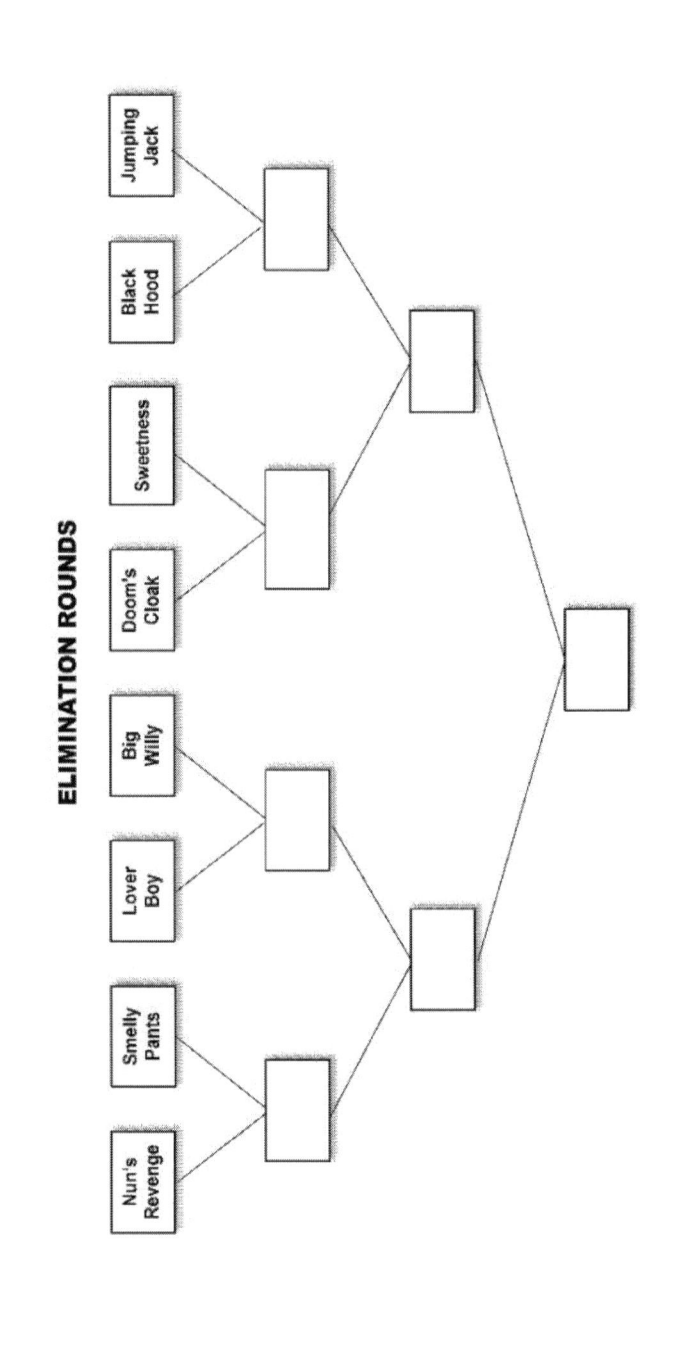

- Jumping Jack
- Black Hood
- Sweetness
- Doom's Cloak
- Big Willy
- Lover Boy
- Smelly Pants
- Nun's Revenge

CHAPTER 15

Nun's Revenge -v- Smelly Pants

The Avatar Smelly Pants knows he must be quiet in this forest.

He's already encountered a stinging monster and dispatched that with a deft swing of his sword. He now has to find a way to cross a river with flesh eating fish lurking in the depths of the water, unseen until the water is disturbed by an unsuspecting swimmer. The thing to do, Smelly decides, is to find a place to cross that is not only shallow, but also narrow. That way he can make a dash for the other side and avoid the flesh eating fish.

Quietly creeping along the riverbank, he doesn't notice Nun's Revenge shadowing him.

Nun's Revenge, a female Avatar, had heard the commotion when Smelly had dispatched the stinging monster. She heard the monster's screech in pain as Smelly thrust his sword into its body, and she crept through the trees to investigate. She watched as Smelly cut off the monster's head with a swipe of his sword. Nun's Revenge now knew just how expert Smelly was with that sword and she decided that the discretion of quietly following Smelly was the better part of valour until there was a chance to make a surprise attack on him. If she could kill Smelly she would be able to use Smelly's magic sword.

Smelly followed the river for many miles, dispatching several monsters along the way. This was good news for Nun's Revenge. The more monsters that Smelly could kill, the less monsters for her to tackle, with an added bonus that the magic sword is being made more powerful with each kill.

Several times, Smelly stopped to listen to the noises of the forest. He was pretty sure he was being stalked, but each time he turned round he saw nothing but trees. With a shrug of his shoulders, he continued his path along the riverbank. He was hungry, and thirsty, but sustenance would have to wait until he was safely across the river. Perhaps he could find a place to pitch his bivouac for the night. Somewhere private, and quiet, and hidden.

Late in the afternoon he was beginning to lose hope of crossing the river. Tired and hungry he was beginning to think that perhaps it was time to bivouac down, do some fishing for his tea and bed down to rest for the remainder of the day. Tomorrow promised to be a more taxing day to travel and he would need as much rest as he could get if he had any chance of winning the top prize for his owner. He wondered what the flesh eating fish would taste like.

Looking for a suitable place to pitch his tent he heard a low rumble. It was a constant sound, different from the gentle bubbling of the river as it flowed over the undulations in its passage downstream. This sound was a menacing sound. A sound that warned of danger. Becoming more alert, Smelly continued along the trail parallel to the river. The rumbling sound got louder with each step. The noise soon masked all noise from the forest.

Smelly's heart pounded inside his chest as he walked along the path. He rounded a bend and, to his surprise and relief, realised that the noise was being made by a waterfall. The river narrowed slightly at the waterfall and disappeared as it tipped over the edge of a precipice. He carefully approached the precipice and peered over the edge. Although this was a convenient place to cross the river he would need to be careful walking over the slippery stones to the opposite river bank. The drop to the bottom of the cliff was long. At least two hundred feet down to where the water crashed onto rocks and exploded into mist that eventually settled and became a new river.

Smelly cautiously backed away from the slippery edge. A drop that big would surely kill him… And that would be the end of his game with nothing to show for his hard work.

He cleared the debris from a suitable patch of ground behind a large boulder, pitched his tent and prepared his sleeping bag for the night. Returning to the river he took a net out of his backpack and caught a couple of flesh eating fish for his tea. Cooking these over his primus he sat next to the river, enjoying his meal and daydreaming about what his owner was going to spend his vast winnings on. His balmy ambiance made him forget about being alert.

After his meal he reflected on how tasty the flesh eating fish were. The taste was something akin to roast potatoes. He washed his plate and utensils in the stream and kneeled down to drink from its clean, cool water. Immersing his face in the water he drank the cooling liquid.

As he raised his face from the river, he saw a reflection of Nun's Revenge standing over him. This was the opportunity Nun's Revenge had patiently been waiting for.

Nun's Revenge punched Smelly, hard, on the side of his head. Too late to take any action to avoid the punch, Smelly fell to his side and kicked out at Nun's Revenge, but missed. Crawling backwards, crab-like to avoid Nun's boot, he grabbed a handful of stones and threw them at Nun. She merely waved these out of the way and continued to follow Smelly's crabwalk, but Smelly was quick. He twisted sideways and rolled over to make sufficient room for him to stand. Facing Nun's Revenge he realised that his trusty sword was lying on his sleeping bag inside his tent. Nun's Revenge charged and propelled a hefty forearm jab into Smelly's chest. This was immediately followed by an uppercut to Smelly's jaw, followed by a straight-arm jab to his nose.

Smelly was unable to avoid this battery of punches. He stumbled backward and found himself on the edge of the precipice. As he struggled to gain a foothold on the slippery rocks, Nun's Revenge took this opportunity to plant a final fist onto his jaw. The momentum of that punch projected Smelly over the edge, where he fell to his death on the rocks far below.

This Avatar's game was over…

ELIMINATION ROUNDS

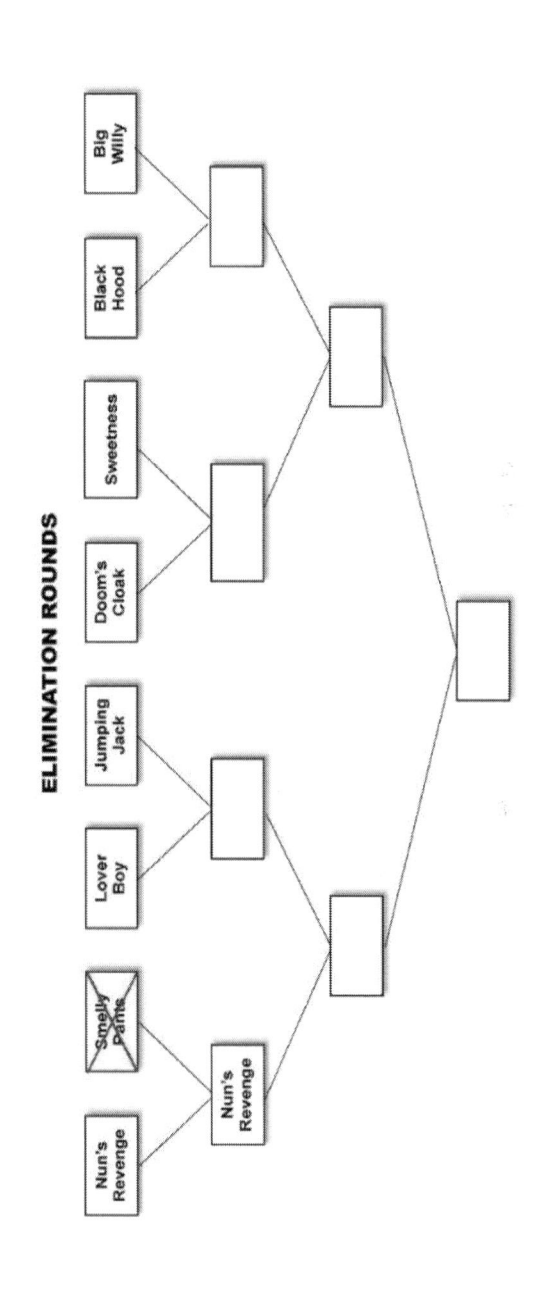

- Nun's Revenge
- Smelly Pants
- Nun's Revenge
- Lover Boy
- Jumping Jack
- Doom's Cloak
- Sweetness
- Black Hood
- Big Willy

John Jackson has had to battle against bad luck for most of his life.

He is an unassuming kind of guy who, some time ago, was dumped on by his former employer until he walked out on his job. Since then, he has been enjoying a peaceful life with his family, working as a warehouse manager.

Getting the warehouse job was a consignment of good luck, assigned to him by some unknown, unseen entity that manipulates people's quota of luck. Right now, however, this entity dispenses bad luck only. Bad luck with a twist.

John relaxes with a bit of on-line gaming during his lunchtime break. He uses his mobile phone, tapping the App for his game of 'LUCKY, OR WHAT?'

He found this game while doing an internet search of games to play on his phone, and he has been playing the game for quite some time. He's been lucky enough to become one of the eight finalists, and he has declined the award of a two hundred and fifty-thousand pound prize to go on to try and win the top prize of four million pounds.

That sum is a life changer, but so is losing the game…

He sighed a long and disappointed sigh. He had just lost the game, he had lost his deposit and he had lost his award of two hundred and fifty-thousand pounds. If only he had accepted the award when he had had the chance.

He was more disappointed that he had not worked his Avatar to put up much of a fight, but then he had stupidly left the Avatar's magic sword in its tent when he sent it down to the stream to wash up. He should have realised that it is fatal to lower your guard at any time during this game.

'Oh well,' he thought, *'I can always start again with a new game.'*

Wrong!

John put his phone away, screwed up his lunch bag and prepared to get back to work. A message was put out over the warehouse tannoy.

"John Jackson. Please come to the office" the tannoy shouted.

Wondering why he had been summoned to the office, he quickened his pace and took the stairs to the office mezzanine two at a time. Entering the office he found chaos. The staff were hurriedly trying to move equipment and filing cabinets away from a corner of the ceiling that had water dripping from it. John mucked in and helped his staff move the equipment and files to a safer place. When everyone was happy that the office contents were safe they stood back and surveyed the ceiling. It had sagged, and a hole about six inches in diameter had opened up from which the dirty water was dripping. Glancing out of the window John noticed the rain lashing down.

"Looks like the roof is leaking," one of the staff offered.

"Are you joking?" replied John, with a wry smile at the woman.

The woman lowered her head in embarrassment at making such an obvious statement. John's brain engaged and he gave instructions to the staff.

"Get on to Head Office and let them know what has happened" to one person. "Ask the Facilities Manager to come upstairs and meet me on the roof" to another.

He then made his way to the roof.

On his way up the roof stairs, he heard the rain beating down onto the corrugated roof sheets above. The low rumble of the rain on the roof got louder the higher he climbed. When he reached the roof door he pushed the bar to release its lock and opened the door about twelve inches to peer outside. The rain was almost horizontal, indicating a heavy wind. John decided to wait until the FM arrived before venturing out onto the roof to see where the water was entering the building. He cursed himself for not putting a raincoat on before coming up to the roof.

The FM arrived about five minutes after John. He had dressed ready to brave the wind and rain. John followed him onto the roof, his shirt immediately soaking through to his body. The FM found the source of the water ingress straight away. It was a blocked gutter. The volume of rain water running into the gutter was clearly too much for it to cope and the water overflowed through the eaves of the roof into the building.

"I'll get a builder to clear it out," shouted the FM, above the sound of the wind and rain.

"If we clear the gutter, will that stop the water?" John shouted back.

"Yes, probably, But we'll still need a builder to re-align the gutter and close the gap in the eaves."

"How long?" asked John.

"It'll probably be a couple of days before a builder can call. They'll all be busy right now looking at storm damage."

"That's no good." shrugged John. "The water will run into the main warehouse area and cause a lot of product damage. We need to do something now."

"It's too dangerous, John. We need scaffold to get to the gutter. It's not possible from the roof."

"Nothing's impossible, Frank. Go get me a large plastic bag to stuff into the eaves. I'll tackle the blockage."

"Don't John. Health and Safety will go ballistic if they know we've ventured over the safety barrier."

"Sod them. I'm not letting our products go to ruin over a bit of rain. Go get that plastic bag."

With a sigh the FM made for the roof door, holding onto the barrier rail to brace himself against the wind. John dipped his head under the barrier rail and climbed out to stand on the edge of the roof. He peered over the precipice - a long way down!

Holding tightly onto the barrier rail with his right hand he lowered himself onto his one knee and reached down to the gutter. Unable to reach it, he straightened the arm holding the rail to give him a few more inches of distance for his left hand. Still not enough.

'*Okay,*' he thought, '*let's try this.*'

He laid on his stomach, parallel to the gutter, and reached out. At last, he could get his hand into the gutter and clear out all the debris. The wind and rain howled down on top of him, relentlessly drumming on his back and shoulders. The FM reappeared through the roof doorway.

"John! What the hell are you doing?" he shouted. "It's stupid to go out on that side of the barrier, especially without a safety harness. I've brought some tools to clear the gutter from this side."

"Too late," smiled John. "I've already done it."

John pushed himself up, onto his hands and knees, took hold of the barrier rail and started to pull himself upright. He thought how lucky he had been to stem the flow of water into the warehouse before any of the products inside had been ruined.

Entity had other ideas about John's life quota of luck!

As John pulled himself onto one foot, his back to the edge of the roof, the precipice beckoned him. His supporting foot slipped on the slimy roof, his wet hand slipped off the barrier rail and he went over the edge.

Two hundred feet later his body crashed onto the paving below.

John Jackson no longer exists in the real world. His luck had finally run out and he had died in much the same way that his Avatar in the game had died…

PLAYER STATUS

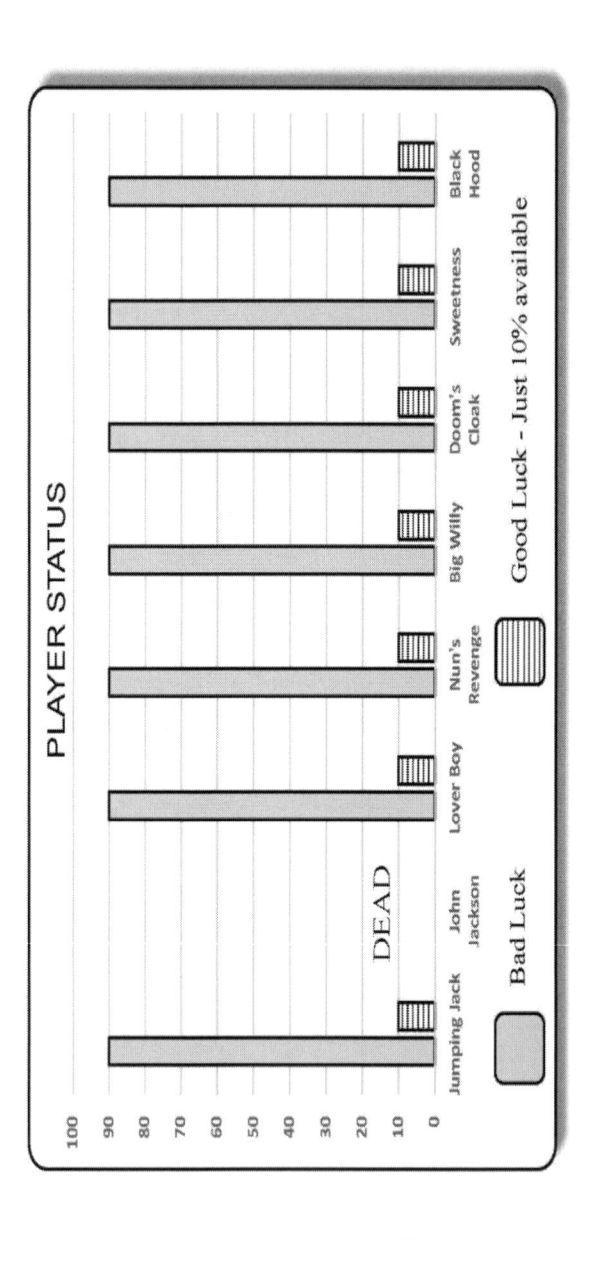

Player	Status
Jumping Jack	90
John Jackson	DEAD
Lover Boy	80
Nun's Revenge	70
Big Willy	70
Doom's Cloak	70
Sweetness	80
Black Hood	90

Bad Luck

Good Luck - Just 10% available

CHAPTER 16

Doom's Cloak -v Sweetness

Doom's Cloak woke up when the sunlight streamed through the cave entrance and slowly crept across the floor until it touched his face. The sun was hot this morning, so Doom packed away his heavy jacket and opted for just a t-shirt.

He knew that exposing his arms to the elements was a dangerous strategy. Apart from sunburn there were numerous tiny bugs and creatures out there that could attach themselves to his skin and inject poison into his veins or bite tiny chunks from him or deposit acid faeces that drills a hole into his muscle. Any one of these hazards could become infected and, with just a small portable medipak, Doom knew that an infection would surely hinder his owner's chances of winning the game. He would just have to inspect his arms frequently to swat away any possible offenders.

Doom's cave is a perfect base. It is situated in a good spot. A commanding position high up, where he can watch the surrounding fields and shrubs for any creatures or Avatars that may stray into his domain. He had been bunked down in the cave for several weeks and he had set up a concealed killing post just outside the entrance. He knew that the creatures and, indeed, Avatars would see the cave entrance and climb the slope to investigate its contents.

All he needed to do was sit in his hide and wait for the targets to come to him. They would never know what hit them.

What Doom didn't realise is that he had been watched by another Avatar for a couple of days while that Avatar formulated a plan to kill Doom. That Avatar is called Sweetness.

Now, Sweetness isn't as sweet as her name suggests. In fact, Sweetness is a devious, underhanded female Avatar intent on winning the big prize for her owner.

One morning, as Sweetness approached a clearing on the edge of the forest, she noticed a cave entrance up ahead. She dropped to the ground, took out her thermal binoculars and peered through the grass to see what, if anything, was using the cave. Caution was merited because there could be anything lurking inside, and most living things in this environment are dangerous. So she decided to 'case the joint' to see if there was anything that could be considered to be a permanent fixture inside the cave. If not, she could use this cave for some R&R. She settled down in anticipation of a long stake-out.

Just before dusk, that evening, a movement outside the cave's entrance caught her eye. She froze. Her heart bounced around the inside of her chest as she spied on the cave's entrance from under a bush about fifty yards away, unmoving, silent, observant... And patient.

Doom's Cloak suddenly appeared from behind a thick bush near the entrance, took a cautionary look around then went into the cave. He didn't see Sweetness stalking him from under the bush some distance from the cave. Sweetness saw the cave's interior light up briefly when Doom prodded his fire into life and put on more wood. Here was an opportunity for her to make a kill, this time a useful kill of another Avatar not a defensive kill of an obnoxious creature. Hopefully, the weather will stay fine tomorrow for her to make her move. But a plan was needed to draw the cave Avatar out into the open. This plan had to be both daring and dangerous.

One of the gadgets that Sweetness possesses is a small gun. This gun is useful only at close range, but it is lethal if its bolt of electricity penetrates thin fabrics. Sweetness had to get close enough to fire the gun at the other Avatar without the electric bolt fading out before it hits a strategic spot.

However, she had noticed that the other Avatar was wearing just a t-shirt. Perfect. Just the opportunity she needed, but somehow she had to get close to him. She waited out another day, by which time her daring plan had been formed in her mind. The plan was, indeed, both daring and dangerous. If she got it wrong she could finish up as a tasty meal for a passing creature or even target practice for the cave Avatar. She waited, patiently, for the other Avatar to bed down for the night.

The following morning Doom sat up, scratched his head, rubbed the sleep from his eyes and peered through the sunlight to see another gloriously sunny, hot day. Yesterday wasn't quite as hot as today, but Doom's hide was nice and shady. He could take a supply of water with him for when he got thirsty. Saves having to reveal his presence by emerging from the hide.

After a hearty breakfast of creature meat, shot and dragged into the cave one night and roasted over the open fire, he stood and stretched, picked up his long-range rifle, checked that it was ready to fire and made his way to the cave's entrance. Peering out he made a detailed inspection of the surroundings and was surprised by the existence of what appeared to be a body in the clearing just in front of the cave's slope. It was another Avatar. That wasn't there last night when he checked the area before bedding down.

Returning to his back pack he took out his binoculars and crawled to the cave's entrance. Peering through the binoculars he could see that the lifeless Avatar was laying on its stomach with one arm outstretched, its hand empty. The other arm was trapped under its body. This could be a trap, although Doom's attention was taken by the patch of blood covering the entirety of the Avatar's exposed back. It seemed that that Avatar had either lost a fight with one of the creatures or had, perhaps, been shot in the back by another Avatar, although he never heard anything like the firing of a weapon last night. Taking a closer look, Doom noticed the dead Avatar's clothes had been ripped from its upper torso. Doom decided that the damage had been caused by a creature, but also decided to play safe by keeping a watch on the body for the time being. If an opposing Avatar is in the area he didn't need to show himself just yet.

Doom waited out the day, and the following night. He slept little that night, deciding to stay alert for anything that might want to investigate his cave. The following morning was, once more, a beautifully sunny day. He cautiously peered out of the cave and saw the dead Avatar still in the clearing. It hadn't moved since the last time he had laid eyes on it. Better to be safe and give it another twenty-four hours, just in case anyone is watching.

Once more, Doom stayed awake throughout the night. The darkness of the night concealed the dead Avatar, but in the morning it was still there, lifeless, unmoved, motionless. It was now two days and two nights that the dead Avatar had lain there. The flies buzzed around the body in their hundreds, many landing on it to feed on the blood that stained its back. Surely, it was safe to investigate. Perhaps there was something on the body that Doom could use in the future? A weapon, or a shield or even some decent armour.

Doom made his mind up. He couldn't stay cooped up in this cave forever. He had to get out to find food and to bathe in the river - it's been a while now and he was beginning to smell like a wet dog and feel a bit uncomfortable down below - and, importantly, he had a job to do… Find the other Avatars and finish this game.

Picking up his trusty rifle he took one last cautious look around and ventured out into the sun. He brazenly stood in front of the cave entrance for a few seconds. If anyone was waiting for him to emerge now would be the time to pounce. Nothing. The only sounds he heard were the sounds of the forest. He was sure it was safe to investigate the corpse.

Unfortunately, he committed the cardinal sin. He went out into the unknown without wearing his heavy jacket. The jacket had protected him from all sorts of attacks. It was made of a material that reflected bullets, arrows, stones, needles and, indeed, the teeth of some hungry creature. It was a good jacket, one that he had won from an earlier round… But he had left it on his bed in the cave.

With far too much confidence he approached the corpse and stood over it. Taking one last look around he lowered himself onto one knee at the side of the corpse, put his rifle on the ground and waved all the flies away. Distracted by the flies, it didn't occur to him to look for the injury that had caused so much blood to escape, although he noted the pits in the Avatar's skin that had been created by acid faeces bugs. He recollected seeing some creatures lurking on the outskirts of the forest several nights ago. Indeed, he had killed and cooked one of them for his breakfast. Perhaps they had smelled the blood of his kill and had ambushed and overcome this Avatar?

He searched the Avatar's belt for weapons. There were none. He removed the Avatar's watch from its outstretched arm, inspected it and shoved it into his pocket. The Avatar's own pockets didn't have anything in them, so Doom rolled the Avatar over for another inspection.

As Sweetness rolled onto her back her trapped arm was exposed. In her hand she held her electric bolt gun. Doom saw this and stiffened as he watched Sweetness's eyes open and her face smile.

"You bitch!" he snarled and made a sudden move for his rifle. Too late. Sweetness raised her gun and shot him in the centre of his chest. The electric bolt from the gun easily penetrated Doom's thin t-shirt and electrocuted him. He fell back, lifeless, eyes half open, unseeing... Dead.

This Avatar's game was over...

ELIMINATION ROUNDS

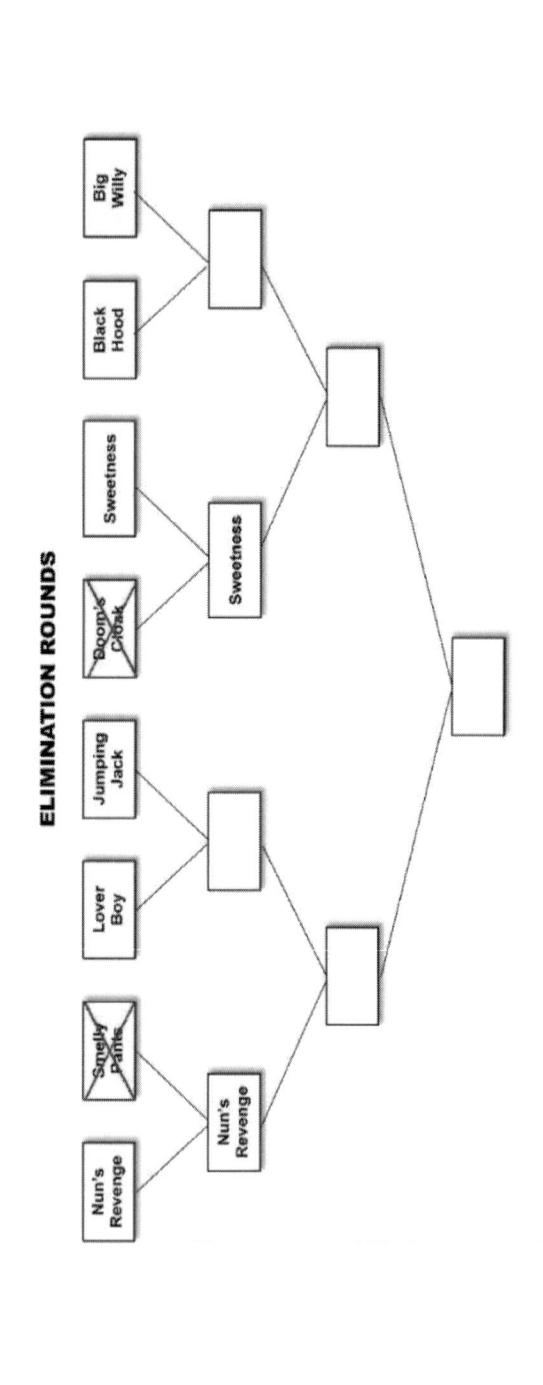

- Nun's Revenge
- Smelly Pants
- Lover Boy
- Jumping Jack
- Sweetness
- Doom's Cloak
- Black Hood
- Big Willy

Round 2:
- Nun's Revenge
- Sweetness

Although Lorenzo (Lory) Enzo had lost his on-line game last night, he was feeling pleased with himself today.

He has just secured a really lucrative contract with a film studio to provide meals for the cast and film-makers for the duration of this filming session. He'd been promised that if he did a good job his contract with this particular film studio would be guaranteed for future films.

He briefed his staff accordingly and instructed his secretary to contact the local labour office for a list of potential new employees to augment his already large workforce. He would need extra staff to service the film contract and they would need to be trained up to an appropriate standard before being let loose on the unsuspecting actors. In the meantime his existing staff will need to work double shifts. He sat in his office to make plans for the supply of food for the studio menus.

Because he had lost the game to a devious female Avatar in the early hours of the morning, thoughts of the four million pound prize had now been removed from his head. '*I don't need the prize, anyway,*' he contemplated. His partnership was thriving and he enjoyed his work, so why did he need a shed load of money to make him happy? He was happy enough now, and as long as things stayed as they are he would remain happy.

Entity had other ideas for Lory's future…

Ten potential waiters/waitresses were sent from the labour office. Although he needed only six, Lory interviewed all ten applicants and sat down with his sous chef - his son - to discuss which of them he should employ. An appropriate selection was made and Lory then instructed his secretary to discharge the rest, making sure that the losers receive a free meal voucher for their troubles.

A week later staff training began.

*

Five percent of Lory's allocated good luck had been used up finishing the game, but Entity had not yet figured out how to deplete Lory's remaining five percent good luck. It wasn't long before an opportunity materialised.

One of the trainees had been given the task of keeping the kitchen clean. As soon as a surface had been used it needed cleaning and disinfecting, and all utensils used in that particular exercise needed washing and sterilising. Lory was fastidious about restaurant cleanliness, especially after his partner's restaurant had been dragged through the mud by a politician.

One evening, before leaving work, the trainee enthusiastically mopped the kitchen floor. He knew he was being watched by the sous chef, preparing tomorrow's menus, so the trainee made sure that he did a good job. Vigorously pushing the mop under a work table she accidentally bashed a water pipe running along the wall under the table. Without realising it, she had loosened a connection in the pipe and water began to spurt from the disturbed pipe connection. Nobody noticed the water slowly oozing across the floor because they had all left the restaurant for the night.

The following morning the floor of the kitchen and restaurant was covered with about an inch of water.

Lory was the first to arrive. He uttered profanities under his breath as he sloshed through the restaurant into the kitchen. The establishment will be out of action until the place has been cleaned up. His staff arrived shortly after him. They were immediately instructed to find the source of the water leak and everyone set about searching inside cupboards and behind units. Some were instructed to begin sweeping the water out of the restaurant door. If necessary, the staff can paddle around in a bit of water but the eating area had to be ready for the restaurant's lunch-time customers.

The leak was not discovered during the staff's first inspection. It was obvious that a pipe was leaking somewhere below the worktops, but much work had to be done before full concentration was put to discovering where the water was coming from.

It took the staff about an hour to sweep out the excess water. Dehumidifiers were brought in to dry the eating area, windows were opened to air the place and the staff went about their business preparing lunch.

A slow flow of water continued to annoy the kitchen staff, so everyone concluded that that the leak was under one of the worktops.

A bundle of towels were rolled up and placed across the kitchen threshold to stop the eating area being flooded and the newbie-in-training was instructed to keep the depth of water in the kitchen to a minimum. He spent the day mopping into a bucket and chucking the water out of the back door. Despite the abundance of electrical items in the kitchen, everyone agreed that they would be safe as long as they wore rubber gloves, which they should be doing anyway. After all, the water was now being controlled at about two millimetres in depth.

A system of serving was devised whereby none of the waiters/waitresses were allowed to venture into the kitchen from the eating area. They had to have the meals passed to them by servers inside the kitchen. Lory handed over all food preparation to his sous chef and continued to search for the leak. It wasn't long before he found it.

It was now well into the lunchtime rush and the kitchen was buzzing with work. Staff were passing meals across the threshold like a well oiled conveyor belt, a chef was busy with his chopping, stirring, tasting and food presentation - presentation is everything - the newbie continued to dry the water off the kitchen floor where staff walked or stood and Lory was on his stomach with a spanner trying to stem the leak.

"Leave it, dad. The plumber will be here soon. He can fix it," encouraged Lory's son.

"The plumber can do a proper job. I just want to stop this flow to free up the guy mopping up," replied Lory, straining to tighten the pipe joint.

Then all hell was let loose.

The pipe joint collapsed and water flowed from an exposed end as if it was a tap filling the sink. Water gushed out, soaking Lory… The bits of him that were not already soaked, anyway. He banged his head on the underside of the worktop in surprise and the sudden jolt of the worktop surprised one of the staff who jumped back, knocking an electric mixer off the table top. The mixer was in use when it got knocked off the table. It smashed onto the floor and immediately lit up the area with an array of sparks, flashes, bangs and fizzes.

There was a scream from Lory, below one of the work tables, and the lights throughout the restaurant flickered and went out. Lory's lights also went out.

He had been fatally electrocuted.

Lorenzo Enzo no longer exists in the real world. His luck had finally run out and he had died in much the same way that his Avatar in the game had died…

PLAYER STATUS

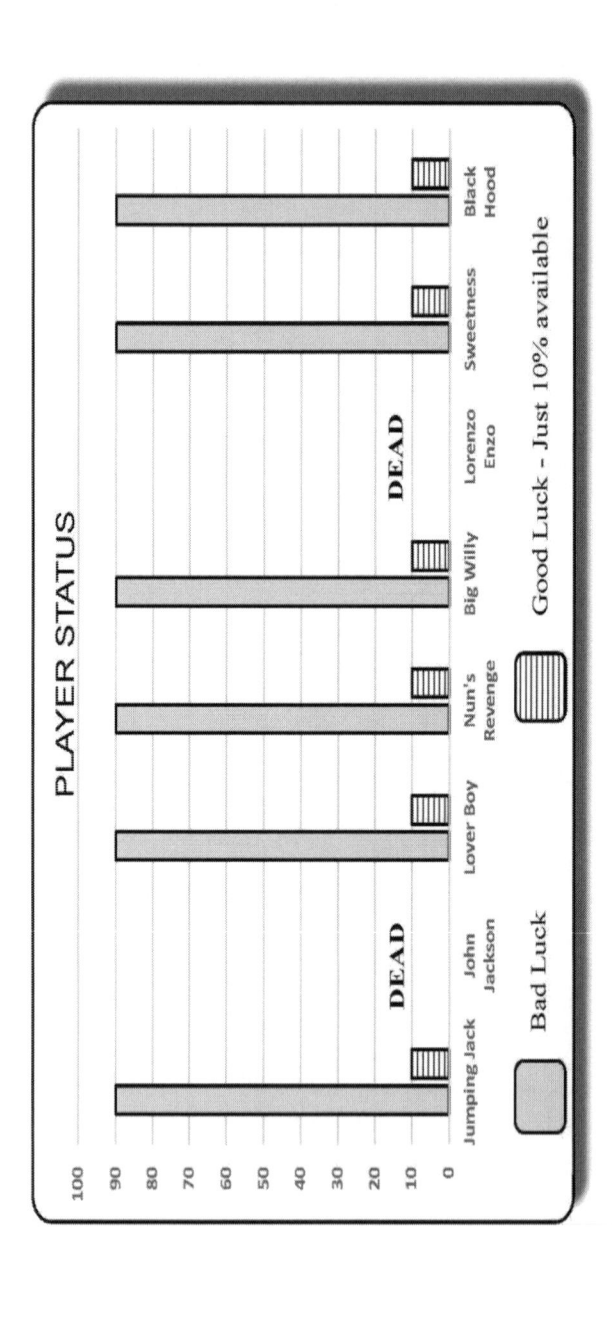

Jumping Jack	John Jackson	Lover Boy	Nun's Revenge	Big Willy	Lorenzo Enzo	Sweetness	Black Hood
~90	DEAD	~90	~10	~80	DEAD	~80	~85

Bad Luck

Good Luck - Just 10% available

CHAPTER 17

Jumping Jack -v- Lover Boy

The hot sun is high in the sky, there is a gentle breeze in the air and the water is calm and flat with a mirror-like surface. All is well with the Avatar Jumping Jack (JJ).

While casually eating his breakfast of scrambled creature eggs with slices of creature belly, JJ is sitting on the shore admiring the raft he had constructed. The overnight spot chosen by him as a hide is secluded, hidden by trees and bushes. He had had no problems getting some well earned zeds after constructing the raft.

He needed the raft to get to an island about a mile out to sea. He was sure there was another Avatar on the island because he had seen the glow of a camp fire during the night. Maybe that Avatar had some useful weapons that he could appropriate, or perhaps it had some upgraded armour. Either way, the time and effort taken to construct the raft would be worth it just to eliminate the other Avatar so as to be closer to pocketing that delicious four million pound pot for his owner.

After burying the creature's carcass and rinsing his hands in the sea he untied the raft's mooring rope and began to paddle, kayak style, for the island. There were two thoughts in JJ's mind as he paddled. The first was *'How did that Avatar get across to the island without being torn apart* by those aquatic creatures with long, sharp teeth and webbed claws that he knew were following his own raft.'* He had seen one of these aquatic creatures tear apart another, much larger, marine creature and he didn't fancy taking on the thing that did the tearing. His second thought was more worrying. *'I hope this raft is good enough for the journey, because I can't swim!'*

It took him forty-five minutes to paddle the distance across the sea, but the raft held together and he breathed a sigh of relief when he finally stepped onto dry land.

*

Lover Boy (LB) had also constructed a raft to get to the island. He had hidden this from view under some bushes in the scrubland before lighting his fire. Being a shrewd planner, he thought *'Why go to the trouble of searching for other Avatars when they will come to me?'* All he needed to do was to advertise the fact that there was an Avatar on the island, and someone would eventually come to investigate.

He was right about that. If he chose his time to attack sensibly, his opponent may well be tired from the journey across the sea and be easily overwhelmed. Anyway, he could use some well earned R&R. The journey to this stage of the game had been long and arduous and he could relax while waiting for someone to get interested in his bonfire.

From behind the sandbank he saw that his bait had been taken. All he had to do was wait for his next kill to arrive. In the meantime, he would need to formulate a plan.

*

JJ had decided not to approach the island head on. Instead, he paddled around it to land on a beach on the other side of a peninsular sticking out to the right of the island. With a bit of luck he could creep up on whoever had stupidly advertised his presence.

Crouching down to tie the raft's mooring rope to a rock he cautiously peered over the rocks to see if he had been detected by the other Avatar while paddling across the sea. Nothing. No movement, no sign of the other Avatar. A stalk through the scrubland looks like the best way to creep up on it.

*

LB had come up with a brilliant plan. One that didn't involve a fight. Why go to the trouble of fighting, with every chance of being eliminated, when one could engineer a way of getting the opposing Avatar to eliminate itself?

He chose a good vantage point behind the sand dune to observe the other Avatar begin its journey across the sea.

If he was right, LB would be presented with just the opportunity he needed to eliminate his opponent. He was right about that, as well.

*

JJ cautiously approached the dying embers of the bonfire.

Making furtive glances all around to ensure that he was alone, he poked the ashes to determine how long the fire had gone unattended. It appeared to have been left dormant for some time. He now had one of two alternatives to choose from; either the opposing Avatar was still on the island and had gone off to find food, or it had departed from the island some time before he had woken up that morning.

First thoughts - try to find a raft. If a raft was still on the island, so was the Avatar. If there was no raft then the other Avatar must have departed. He searched the area adjacent to the beach. No raft. He then decided to search the forest area, some fifty yards across the scrubland.

*

LB had anticipated JJ's every move.

While JJ had been paddling across the sea LB had dragged his raft from the scrubland back into the forest.

Using his sword he quickly and quietly cut some branches and concealed the raft under sum thickets. He then climbed up into a tree's canopy. Laying on his belly, concealed by the thick canopy of leaves, he kept watch for the other Avatar.

His plan was to let the other Avatar walk by, assuming the raft had not been detected, and wait until the Avatar had disappeared further into the forest. Then LB could make his move to eliminate his opponent.

Either way, all he had to do was wait and be patient. He didn't have long to wait.

*

JJ entered the forest, continually searching for any sound or movement that would reveal the presence of something close by. He had once been surprised by a canny creature that jumped out from behind a wall and he had had quite a battle dispatching it. So the order of the day was to stay alert.

When searching through forests, it's a common mistake not to search upwards. It's all too easy to think that you will be attacked from behind a tree, or a bush, or from a ditch, but you never think to check the tree tops, do you? LB counted on this and smiled as JJ walked directly under the tree he was hiding in and continued on into the forest in search of something to attack.

JJ spent the next three hours searching the forest but found nothing. No raft, no Avatar, no creatures. Nothing. He was now fairly sure that whoever had lit the bonfire the previous night had departed from the island, unseen. Ah well. Nothing for it but to return to the mainland and continue the search for Avatars to eliminate from there.

He made his way back to his raft, not knowing that LB had been busy while he was in the forest. Taking one last look around JJ launched the raft and began his arduous paddle back to the mainland. He got about halfway across the sea when he noticed one of the rope ties trailing in the water alongside the raft. That worried him. If the ropes were coming loose he might have a problem staying afloat. Knowing that he couldn't swim, he paddled with more enthusiasm. More purpose.

The mainland sea shore was still quite a way off, the water was still too deep and he would be far out of his depth if he fell in. He decided to stop paddling and see if the rope was an important one. That thought was a stupid one because he knew that all the ropes binding the raft were important. The trailing rope now worried him immensely.

As he knelt down to investigate the rope his first mistake was not ensuring that his paddle was safe. This was placed on the raft at the side of him and as he lowered himself down he knocked it into the sea. He made a frantic attempt to retrieve the paddle but got nowhere. The more he splashed around with his hands, the further the paddle floated away from the raft.

Then he noticed something even more disturbing. The raft was beginning to disintegrate! The loose, trailing rope was the one that bound all the raft's floor logs together and these were slowly coming apart. Panic set in and JJ started to thrash around the raft in an attempt to keep himself afloat by trying to hold the logs together.

He then looked behind him to see how far he was away from the island. Too far, and still quite a way to the mainland. In between him and the island he saw LB paddling towards him. *'Perhaps,'* he thought, *'that Avatar is coming to help?'* but he knew that that was a forlorn hope. After all, the idea of the game was to eliminate your opponents. He also noticed one of the aquatic creatures with long, sharp teeth and webbed claws stalking his raft.

*

LB smiled as he saw JJ struggling to stay afloat.

His plan had worked perfectly. When JJ had disappeared into the forest LB had waited until he was sure that JJ would not see him. He then lowered himself down, quietly made his way to JJ's raft and untied the rope binding the floor logs together. He gauged JJ would be well under way before the raft would disintegrate, leaving JJ floating helplessly in the sea. LB's intention was to paddle up to JJ and dispatch him there and then. He didn't know that JJ couldn't swim, but as he paddled closer he saw JJ desperately trying to stay afloat using one of the disintegrated raft's logs.

A single log was unsuitable for such a task, and JJ disappeared below the surface.

Unable to swim, Jumping Jack had possibly drowned... Or had been torn apart by an aquatic creature with long, sharp teeth and webbed claws that followed the raft.

LB looked on as a red stain appeared below the waves and he knew that JJ had been eliminated.

This Avatar's game was over...

ELIMINATION ROUNDS

- Nun's Revenge
- ~~Smelly Pants~~
  - Nun's Revenge
- Lover Boy
- ~~Jumping Jack~~
  - Lover Boy
- ~~Doom's Cloak~~
- Sweetness
  - Sweetness
- Black Hood
- Big Willy

"Damn it!" June Gracey cursed aloud as the on-line game she had been playing had just booted her out of the game play.

"*How annoying…*" she thought to herself. Right now, she would have welcomed the game's pay-out of four million pounds, but she sat back into her deck chair to reflect on her stupidity.

Stupidity not as far as the game was concerned, but stupidity for wasting almost all of the one million pound premium bond win she had frittered away on a life of luxury and partying. She was down to her last fifty-five thousand pounds. That amount of money might be a lot to most of us, but to June it was almost pocket money.

June thought back to five years ago.

Back then she was going through a bad patch. More bad luck than anyone should have had.

Her husband had left her and disappeared with some floozy, leaving June to cope with a load of debt. She'd had to juggle several jobs just to stay afloat.

Just as she thought that her bad luck could not get any worse, it did. Her toddler wrecked the lounge of a house that June was cleaning. Despite offering to pay for the damage, even though she knew that she couldn't afford it, she was sued by the home owner.

Then her luck changed. It had been reset by an unseen entity, whose job it was to monitor everyone's good luck. She won the top premium bond prize of one million pounds. This was June's life changer.

She could now afford to settle the neighbour's law suit, pay off her mortgage, gift a load to her eldest daughter so that she could remain at university, stop working as a skivvy for her neighbours and, after all that, she had enough to buy a motor yacht and sail around the world.

She lived the high life wherever she moored up, drinking, partying and dating almost any bloke she met. Presently, her yacht was free floating about one mile off the coast of Australia while she enjoyed a drink But she now knew that she was running out of money. With her youngest daughter, now seven years old, in an expensive boarding school she had to seriously think about augmenting her money pot, hence the decision to play the game and win that four million pounds. Surely, that amount would see her well off, well into the future.

But she had just lost to someone she had never met and is never likely to meet. Infuriating, eh?

It had taken June several months to reach the finalists level in the game. She realised, when she first started playing the game, that her cash reserves would continue to diminish, but if she could win the prize she would manage her money better and still live a life of luxury.

What she didn't realise is that the previously benevolent entity had now morphed into its dark phase, and this particular entity does not take prisoners!

Something else that she reflected on was the foolishness of living on a boat when you can't swim! But that wasn't so much of a problem, with lots of life jackets scattered around the boat. The worse thing she thought about was being cast afloat in the ocean surrounded by lots of creatures looking for an easy meal, especially the sharks that she had seen circling the boat.

Putting her iPad down, she dozed in the warm Australian sun. It wasn't long before she was fast asleep. She dreamt of the time she had had since boarding her yacht in Southampton, steering it passed the Isle-of-Wight into the English Channel and out into the Atlantic Ocean.

Her dream reminisced about her trip down the coast of Africa to Liberia, turning west to navigate across the Atlantic ocean to Brazil, through the Panama Canal and across the Pacific ocean to Australia. It had taken her five years, during which she had visited many foreign parts and met and slept with many foreign men. But now the good times were over because she had lost the game.

She was rudely woken by a violent bump on the boat's hull. Making a cursory glance around she couldn't immediately see anything that would have caused the boat to jolt. Then she noticed a whale about two hundred yards away, regally undulating in the calm waters of the sea. Perhaps the boat had got in the way of a whale that was not paying attention to its surroundings? Who knows? But a quick look in the cabin didn't immediately reveal any problems, so June returned to her slumber.

It was about one and a half hours later that June's life went pear shaped, helped, no doubt, by the dark web entity. She was again woken, this time by the feel of water lapping around her bare feet. Half awake, half asleep, she looked around to see what had disturbed her slumber. As soon as she realised that the deck was under about an inch of water she jumped up and dashed towards the cabin. It was fully submerged so she knew that the radio was out of action.

In a mad panic she looked around for a life jacket and found one hanging close to her deck chair. Quickly donning the life jacket and tying the cords she frantically scanned the horizon for any other boats that might be in the area. She noticed that her own boat had drifted from the Australian coast which was now more than ten or fifteen miles away, a speck far away on the horizon.

The water covering the deck was now about six inches deep. Whatever had bumped into the boat earlier had cracked its flimsy hull and water was flowing through the damage. The boat was sinking.

June cursed her luck. If only she had carried out a more detailed inspection down below she might have seen the damage and taken steps to repair it. Too late now, though. Her drink induced sleep had let the boat sink past the point of no return.

Frantically scanning the ocean she noticed another yacht about three miles off her port bow. Quickly retrieving a flare gun from one of the deck lockers she primed it, pointed it skyward and pulled the trigger. The flare shot up and exploded into a shower of sparks and smoke high up in the sky. June looked out to the other yacht to see if it had noticed the flare, but it was too far away to see if it had turned towards her. She loaded another flare and shot this into the sky. Then she saw a flare that had been let off by the other boat in response to hers.

With a sigh of relief June looked down at the submerged deck, now knee deep in water. Would the other boat make it to her in time?

To buy time, June climbed onto the roof of the boat and watched as the other one chugged towards her. It was now about a mile and a half away. The deck water was now waist deep.

After about fifteen minutes the rescue boat had motored to about three quarters of a mile away from June. The deck water was now lapping over the gunwales and the boat was sinking much faster. June prayed that she would have enough time to be rescued before the boat fully sank, but it was looking unlikely.

The rescue boat was now about five hundred yards away. The ocean water was up to the underside of the boat's roof.

The recue boat managed to get within twenty yards of June when her own boat succumbed to the pull of the deep. June was left free floating as the rescue boat finally got to within a few feet of her. A hand went down to pull her from the water but a large shark that had been following the boat got to her first.

June was dragged down to the dark depths, and her blood stained the ocean red.

June Gracey no longer exists in the real world. Her luck had finally run out and she had died in much the same way that her Avatar in the game had died…

PLAYER STATUS

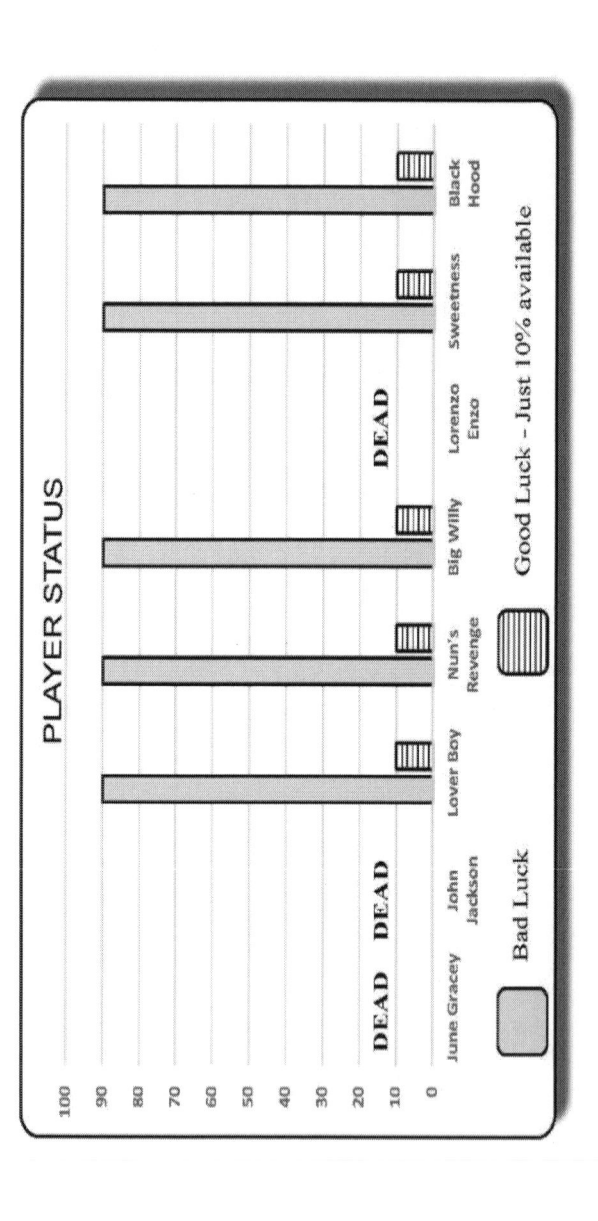

Player	Status
June Gracey	DEAD
John Jackson	DEAD
Lover Boy	~95
Nun's Revenge	~15
Big Willy	~15
Lorenzo Enzo	DEAD
Sweetness	~80
Black Hood	~90

Bad Luck

Good Luck - Just 10% available

CHAPTER 18

Big Willy -v- Black Hood

The weather is atrocious today. The temperature has dropped to -20°C and sleet is falling like vertical stair rods - really lashing down. Nobody is venturing out of their hides until the weather improves. Even the creatures huddle down in their burrows to shelter from the storm.

*

At this stage we should digress from the game to explain what is happening in the real world. The world away from the dark web game.

The game's inventor originally published the interactive internet game to earn some pocket money. As it turns out the game, you'll recall, netted him a goodly sum of two hundred million pounds.

The inventor initially thought he could sit back and let the money roll in, but he was wrong.

The game's platform required a high degree of maintenance, as do all internet games, so the inventor spends a lot of his time debugging problems, re-designing screens, improving the Avatars and generally keeping the game oiled and smooth running. But the game has stopped working.

From the player's perspective the game has frozen.

What the inventor has never realised is that the game has been illicitly hijacked by a dark web entity, who controls the allocation of luck to all players. I'm sure that you have all, by now, picked up on the fact that what happens to the player's Avatar in the game is reflected in their real world activities… How they are eliminated in the game is loosely mirrored in their real life. The game's inventor doesn't know this. If he knew this he would, surely, shut the game down… Wouldn't he?

Anyway, one should assume that whatever happens to the players in real life will also be reflected in the game. This is Entity's influence on both the players and their Avatar.

So… The storm that is taking place in the game is also happening in the real world. The real world has now entered its winter period and all sorts of bad weather is affecting people's travel arrangements. In the dark depths of the north pole the real world is cloaked in darkness for months during its winter period, and the people who live and work there are shrouded in darkness for the winter months. Entity has engineered a similar effect within the game.

As far as the game's inventor is concerned, the delay in the game was due to a glitch that needed fixing. Otherwise, players will become unhappy and start asking for their deposit back. This will not be a good thing, will it? So the inventor has temporarily paused the game to carry out important maintenance.

It took the game's inventor several days to find a fix for his program bug. More than a week!

Eventually, the only thing he could think of was to relocate the game to a different cloud on the internet. Having carried out a laborious series of checks and double checks he was finally satisfied that he could un-pause the game for the players to continue their trek for that top prize of four million pounds.

The inventor's days of debugging the game translated to weeks for the Avatars.

Back to the game…

*

It has now been several weeks since any of the Avatars had ventured out of their hides.

Fortunately, they had all stocked up on creature meat when the weather started to turn against them. All, that is, except Big Willy.

It is important to know that in this game's Avatars are all carnivores. Pure meat-eaters. Kids in the real world are very much the same. They don't like greens, do they? Not cabbage, not sprouts, not cauliflower, not broccoli. They prefer sausages and burgers, don't they?

The Avatars are very much like kids. They resist eating any kind of vegetation, not least because some of it is poisonous. Some nuts are safe, but most Avatars stay away from anything with roots.

Because Willy didn't have the foresight to stock up on meat before the storm took hold he ran out of food relatively early on. So it has now been almost two weeks since he had had any opportunity to look for food. He tried a hunting spree after the first few days of incarceration, but this proved to be abortive. A mere one hour outside in this weather and he realised that all the creatures had disappeared into their burrows and he would have frozen to death searching for them, so he returned to his cave and waited out the storm.

Just before the storm broke, Black Hood (BH) saw Willy creeping through the forest. He stalked Willy for days, waiting for the chance to shoot an arrow into him. He missed that chance when the dark clouds opened up and pelted everything with piercing sleet. Nothing for it but to bunker down in a hide and wait for Willy to show himself.

During Willy's foray outside the cave for food he almost crashed into BH's hide. He missed the tangle of branches by just a couple of yards but didn't see the hide's shape. He walked past, not realising that another Avatar was hiding in the thicket. If BH had been on his guard, he would have realised that Willy had just walked past his hide. As it is, however, BH was sleeping in his nice warm sleeping bag.

Willy's disturbance of the undergrowth as he walked past the hide woke BH who remained still and quiet, thinking that perhaps a creature, or even another Avatar, was stalking *him*. After Willy had walked by, BH ventured out into the cold to do some stalking of his own.

Willy circled round and began his return to the cave. By the time BH had positioned himself to get a clear shot through the trees it was too late. Willy had reached the cave's entrance. BH shot off a hurried arrow in the hopes that it would find Willy's torso, but it missed by yards and hit the wall at the side of the cave entrance. Willy turned and saw BH priming another arrow so he retreated into the darkness of the cave. BH cursed his stupidity in not attempting an earlier shot.

BH knew that any movement towards the cave, now that he had been detected, would illicit a volley of gun fire from the other Avatar who holds a commanding position. Both Avatars knew that a stand-off was now obvious.

He shouted up at the cave entrance, "You're trapped! Give up now and I'll make your death a quick and painless one. Stay inside and you starve."

Willy didn't reply, but he knew that he would soon need some food.

BH kept watch on the cave's entrance. Two weeks passed by. He shot an occasional arrow into the cave to make sure that Willy knew he was still waiting outside, but Willy remained within the cave's dim confines. He was now desperate for a meal, and he was about to leave the cave and put up a fight when, unpredictably, something really extraordinary happened.

BH had now also run out of food, except for a single creature, held inside a cage in his hide.

He had kept this creature alive by feeding and watering it regularly. Although the weather was now improving, he had not had the opportunity to go hunting because he had needed to keep a constant watch on the cave's entrance to await the appearance of his prey. He cooked the creature, but had no intention of eating it himself.

He shouted up at the cave's entrance, "Okay. You win. I'm cold and tired and fed up with this waiting game. I'm going to look for someone else. You can do what you want, but just remember that our paths will cross again in the future... And you will not be so lucky when that happens."

He walked away from his hide, waving to Willy's cave as he departed. He had left the creature carcass in his pan of stew, bubbling away over an open fire.

Willy peered round the edge of the cave's entrance to watch BH disappear into the forest. Should he trust him? Was that other Avatar on the level? Had he really left me alone?

He decided to give it a few hours to see what happened.

As those hours passed, Willy got a whiff of the meat stew. Boy, was he hungry!

His stomach bubbled at the smell of the cooked meat from BH's abandoned pot of stew. His mouth salivated at the thought of a meal. His hands shook. His legs were weak from lack of food. He knew that he was in no condition to fight, but his hunger overwhelmed any thought of a conflict. Whether the other Avatar was out there, waiting for him or not, he decided that he must go and find the source of the cooked meat. If it meant fighting for it, he would put up as good a fight as his condition would allow.

With an air of resignation he blatantly walked out of the cave and stood in the open, waiting for the inevitable attack. It didn't happen. He looked around, scanning the forest, but heard no sound or saw any movement that would alert him to an attack. Everything was quiet.

With some trepidation he strode out to follow his nose to the meat waiting for him. It didn't take long to find the other Avatar's hide. A pot of stew had been left cooking when the other Avatar had vacated the site. Willy scanned the area and then looked down, into the pot. He bent and smelled its rising vapour. The stew was just too good to be true.

Making one last scrutiny of his surroundings he took out a spoon from his backpack and dipped into the stew.

Willy revelled in his good fortune. The other Avatar had departed and left him this delicious stew. Quite how the other Avatar had made this stew so tasty was anybody's guess. It was smooth and tasty, with a slightly nutty flavour. The meat was perfectly cooked. It must have been sautéed before being put in the pot to stew. *'His loss, my gain,'* thought Willy as he woofed down the meal straight from the pan. Half of the stew had been devoured before Willy's stomach screamed "Enough!" He washed it down with cool water from the nearby stream and sat back to reflect on why the other Avatar had given up so easily.

Then it hit him!

With a sudden dash back to the hide he upturned the pot and looked down at the remnants of the stew. In utter horror he saw what was now giving him the worst stomach cramps he had ever experienced.

"No!" he screamed as he dashed back to the stream for more water. His stomach cramp had now turned into a sinister pain. A bad pain, and he was beginning to feel light headed. He never made it to the stream. He doubled up in pain and dropped to his knees. The pain intensified and the fuzziness in his head turned into a dizziness never before experienced. The forest spun round and round. He was disoriented and in pain and unable to stay upright. He fell forward onto his stomach and pulled his legs up to his chest, in so much pain that he screamed out. He vomited and then looked up to see a shadow standing over him.

Rolling onto his back he looked up at the shadow with eyes that were unable to focus properly. He heard the other Avatar speak to him.

"Ah, I see you found my stew. I left it cooking especially for you. Did you enjoy it?"

No response. The pain in Willy's stomach was now so intense it was impossible to talk.

"Oh dear," smiled BH. "You didn't find those poison berries in the bottom of the pot until it was too late, did you? Never mind. It won't be long now. You will soon be in the hands of your maker and the pain you are now in will be gone."

The last words that Willy heard were the sarcastic utterances of Black Hood. "Shall I say a little prayer for you?"

Willy looked at the sky with sightless eyes. He slowly faded away until he lay there, motionless, dead.

This Avatar's game was over…

ELIMINATION ROUNDS

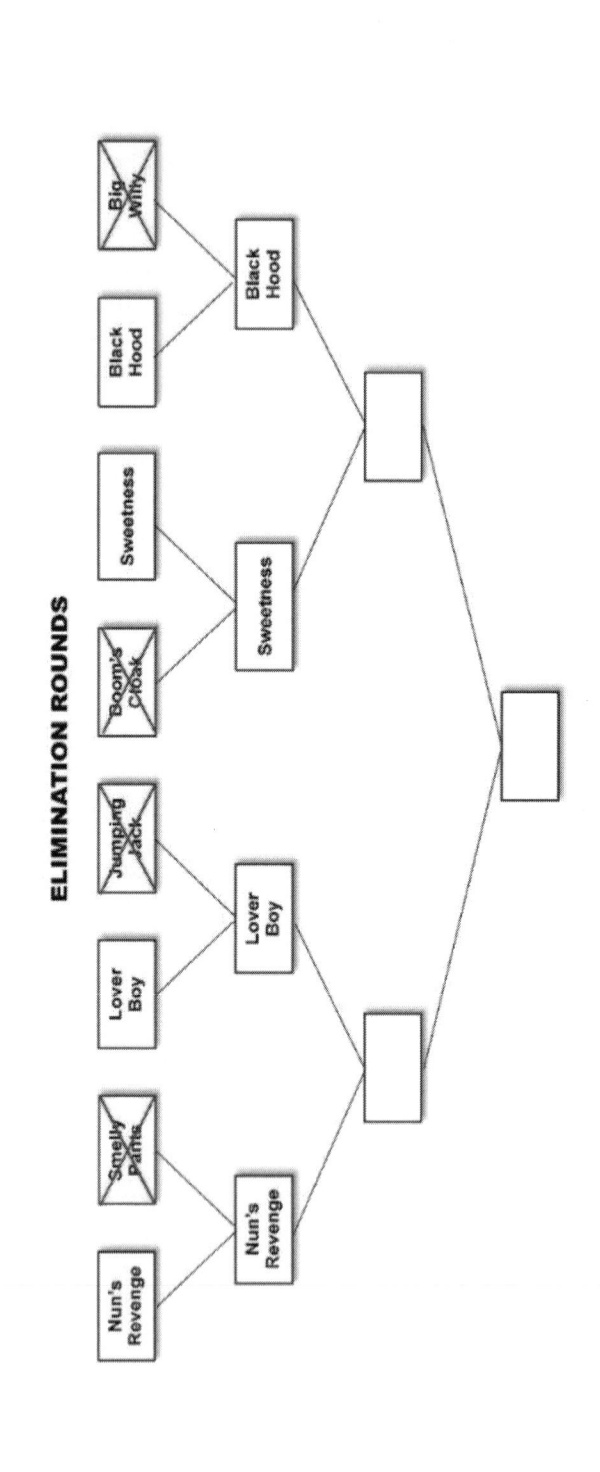

- Nun's Revenge
- Smelly Pants → Nun's Revenge
- Lover Boy
- Jumping Jack → Lover Boy
- Nun's Revenge vs Lover Boy → ?

- Boom's Cloak
- Sweetness → Sweetness
- Black Hood
- Big Willy → Black Hood
- Sweetness vs Black Hood → ?

Final: ?

Enzo Lorenzo's luck, you will recall, went through a bad patch because some stupid politician had cast aspersions about possible food poisoning from his restaurant. Although he sued the politician - and won - social media screwed up his business.

Eni and Lory (aka Doom's Cloak) had discussed this game when it first came out. They both saw their entrance fee as an investment on the basis that if one of them won the game, the partnership would have a cool four million pounds to invest in the business.

Okay… Recently, Eni had read on his social media page that his partner had been eliminated from the game. Killed by a bolt from an opposing Avatar's electric bolt gun.

Eni thought, '*Bad luck. I bet that was painful.*' with a wry smile. He hoped that his own bad luck was not returning to haunt him. It most certainly was!

His own Avatar, Big Willy, has just been eliminated so he kissed the big prize goodbye and opened his mail. One of his letters was from a solicitor in Italy asking him to make contact as soon as possible.

Eni lifted his phone receiver and dialled the solicitor's number. A thought at the back of his mind connected the Italian solicitor with his Italian partner, so maybe establishing contact was important. When he was eventually put through to the solicitor he was given some really disturbing news.

After establishing that Eni was Lory's partner the solicitor declared, gravely, "I'm sorry to have to inform you that your partner died yesterday. He was electrocuted in an accident at his restaurant. Please accept my condolences."

This news hit Eni like a boxer's punch. He sat holding his telephone receiver up to his ear in silence. The solicitor woke him from his thoughts.

"Are you still there, Señor Lorenzo?"

"Oh, yes. Sorry. I was taken aback by the news."

"I will be sending papers to you for your urgent signature," the solicitor advised. "As soon as we have received the papers back in this office I will put steps in motion to transfer all of Signor Enzo's interests in the partnership to you. Do you think you will be retaining this firm to deal with disposal of the restaurant?"

"At this stage, I don't know what I'm going to do. I'll discuss it with my advisor and let you know."

"Of course, Señor Lorenzo. I'll await your reply to my correspondence accordingly and, once more, I am so sorry for your loss."

The call was terminated and Eni sat back to reflect on his next move. He had no idea that Entity had ideas of its own to interfere with his life's luck.

Eni thought it a strange coincidence that Lory had been electrocuted, both in the game and now in real life. He didn't give any thought to his own life's path, and the way he had been eliminated from the game. He had other things on his mind. Who was going to look after Lory's restaurant? Should he travel to Italy now, to sort out the business side of things, or wait until the funeral? There were many more questions to answer.

He was about to telephone Lory's wife when his sous chef poked his head around Eni's office door.

"Señor Aguiñiga is here to see you."

"Aguiñiga? Did he say what he wants?"

"No, chef. He just said he would like to talk to you."

"Okay, send him in."

'*Aguiñiga is the politician that tried to sue me,*' Eni recollected. '*I wonder what he wants now?*'

Aguiñiga strutted into the office and sat down before being invited to sit.

"Good morning Enzo. How are you today?"

"I'm fine, Pablo. How are you?"

Aguiñiga didn't answer Eni's question. "I don't want to take up too much of your time, so I'll come straight to the point. I want to apologise for my actions."

"Oh? Why…? Why now?"

"Well, I know it was a stupid thing to do, on my part, but at the time I couldn't allow those photographs to ruin my career. Okay, you won the lawsuit, but I have now resigned from the government. Had to. I was forced out by the do-gooding party members, and I now want to try to repair our friendship."

Eni wondered what the ex-politician would get out of this renewed friendship, but he was willing to let bygones be bygones and he stood to shake Aguiñiga's hand.

"Let me take you to dinner at my club," offered Aguiñiga. "You can taste the delights of our chef's exclusive menu. What do you say?"

"It's kind of you to offer, Pablo. Yes, I accept your apology, and I accept your invitation."

The two men shook hands, once more, and Aguiñiga left to make the arrangements with Eni's secretary.

Two weeks later Eni donned his best Giorgio Armani suit and made his way to Pablo's club. He was greeted by an attractive woman dressed as a flamenco dancer and escorted to the table where Pablo was waiting for him.

"Hello, my friend," welcomed Pablo. "What would you like to drink?"

At their table the food order was taken by their waiter and the two men talked and stuffed their faces with a superb menu, especially concocted by the club's chef. He came out to introduce himself to Eni.

"It is a huge privilege and honour to serve such a famous chef as yourself." the chef gushed. "I do hope you enjoyed my signature meal."

"It was delicious," answered Eni.

Pablo then ushered Eni to the bar and bid him to sit in one of the plush chairs in front of a low table.

"A night-cap? What would you like?"

Having taken Eni's order, Pablo went to the bar to get the drinks. He returned a couple of minutes later with the two drinks and sat opposite Eni. Eni thought it a bit odd that Pablo had taken the trouble to fetch the drinks personally, especially as there were a couple of waiters flitting about with a tray each, carrying drinks ordered by the occupants of the lounge.

'*Perhaps,*' he thought, '*Pablo just wants to show how sorry he was by making an extra effort for me?*'

The two men sat and chatted about nothing in particular until Eni stood and declared that it was time for him to go home. As he stood up he felt a slight twinge of irritable bowels. Just a hint, but noticeable, nonetheless. He bid Pablo a safe journey home, collected his coat and went out into the cold winter air. It was beginning to rain, a sleety rain that made everyone lean into it, head down.

He waited on a corner, ready to hail a passing taxi. He needn't have bothered. After five minutes of standing there the irritability of his bowels turned to pain, and the pain rapidly increased in intensity. It became so bad that Eni had to drop to his knees, doubled up in agony. He didn't see Pablo casually approaching him from the club.

*

Pablo Aguiñiga, ex-politician, harboured a grudge. Like any narcissistic person of objectionable character, he wrongly blamed Lorenzo's restaurant for making him sick that night, precisely at the time a press photographer was passing by.

He had convinced himself that he had got food poisoning from the "crap food" - his words - that he had been served that night, and now his career was shot. In shreds. He had been called to the Prime Minister's office to account for his actions and, indeed, his seemingly illicit liaison with another MP. A colleague... Someone who was not his wife. Having one's picture of one's self vomiting into the gutter in what had been described as a drunken episode doesn't go down well with the voters and, in addition, an illicit liaison would certainly lose votes. So Pablo Aguiñiga had been persuaded that it was in the party's best interests if he was to resign. He resigned.

His hatred of Lorenzo had influenced his rational thinking and, in an attempt, to claw back some resemblance of dignity he tried to sue Lorenzo and his restaurant, but he had lost the case. Consequently, he was faced with a huge legal bill and the prospect of having to make reparations to Lorenzo for slander and libel. His bank account took a massive hit.

Aguiñiga's hatred of Lorenzo was now at fever pitch and he had to find a way to pay Lorenzo back. After mulling it over, he came up with a plan, assisted, no doubt, by Entity.

He'd had to eat humble pie by going back to the restaurant and apologising to Lorenzo. Whilst at that meeting he invited Lorenzo to his club for a meal. Good! His invitation had been accepted.

He ate more humble pie during the meal by sucking up to Lorenzo whenever the conversation allowed him to. After the meal, which he paid for, much to his chagrin, he went to the bar to fetch some drinks. While at the bar he surreptitiously emptied a sachet of powder into Lorenzo's drink from the sachet previously secreted in his pocket. He had to be careful not to be seen doing this, or his problems would expand exponentially, and he would be in serious trouble.

The powder was a slow acting emetic that he had acquired from a friend of his at the local hospital. What his friend had omitted to tell Aguiñiga was that a few grains of the powder were all that was required to bring on a bout of acute diarrhoea and vomiting… Not the whole packet! Too much of this stuff and it's a killer.

*

A crowd gathered round Eni as he lay on the pavement, writhing in pain. Bodily fluids were exploding from both ends of him at once and the pain that spread over his stomach and bowels was excruciating. Someone brought an umbrella and a blanket to shelter him from the sleet that continued to lash down. An ambulance, someone was told, was about ten minutes away.

A few people tried to comfort him, but Eni couldn't properly focus on the faces that surrounded his body. As he screamed for help, he couldn't help noticing a flash from within the crowd.

'*What the hell…*' he thought. '*Is that somebody taking a photo of me?*'

Through half-closed eyes he peered into the crowd and saw Aguiñiga smiling down at him. Aguiñiga waved his mobile phone in front of him in mock jest and mouthed the words "*remember?*"

Eni realised what Aguiñiga was alluding to. He tried to lift his hand to point to Aguiñiga, and he tried to say his name, but was unable to. He died on the way to hospital.

A post mortem confirmed that he had been poisoned, but the authorities never found precisely who had done this dastardly deed.

To quote a well-known phrase, 'The politician had got away with murder.'

Enzo Lorenzo no longer exists in the real world. His luck had finally run out and he had died in much the same way that his Avatar in the game had died…

PLAYER STATUS

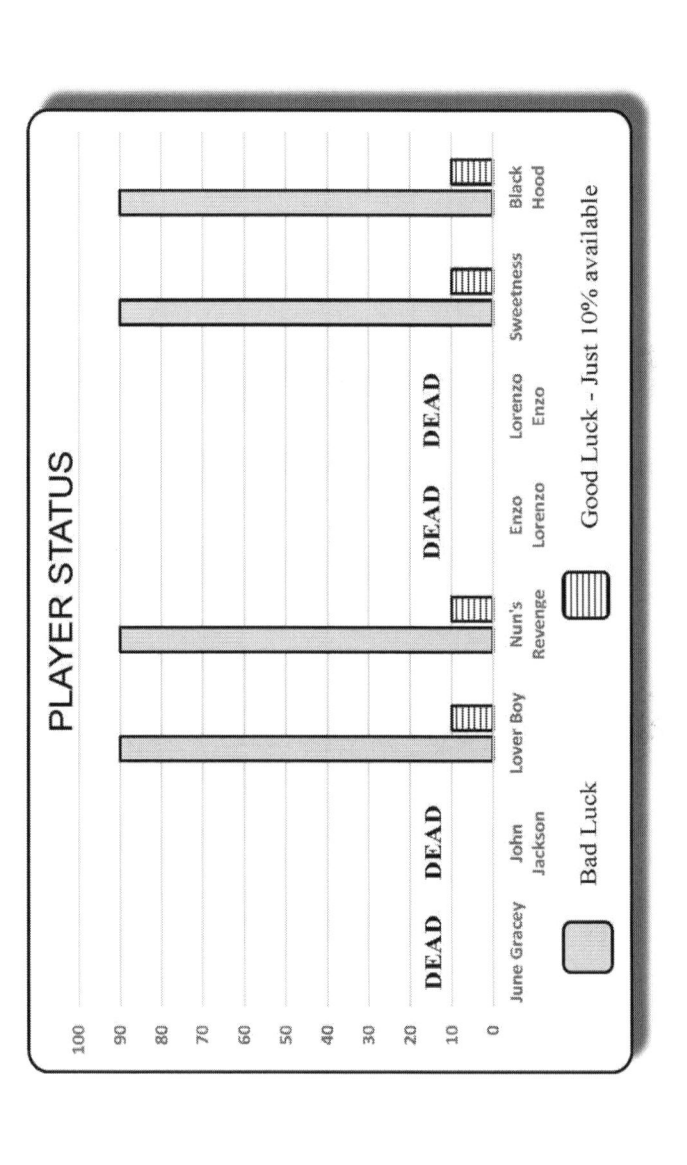

Player	Status
June Gracey	DEAD
John Jackson	DEAD
Lover Boy	90
Nun's Revenge	70
Enzo Lorenzo	DEAD
Lorenzo Enzo	DEAD
Sweetness	90
Black Hood	100

Bad Luck

Good Luck - Just 10% available

CHAPTER 19

Lover Boy -v- Nun's Revenge

A new round in the game is ready to begin.

The four remaining players have all had their breakfasts and limbered up for yet another day of dodging bullets, creatures and each other. They have repaired their Avatar's armour, replenished their Avatar's weapons and made themselves comfortable in front of their gaming consoles.

They have all had their life's luck quota reviewed by Entity and they all now have just three percent of good luck remaining. They don't know it yet, but more of them will soon die.

*

Lover Boy (LB) was still paddling across the sea, having eliminated Jumping Jack. He was pleased with that result. He'd had little to do except loosen a couple of ropes on JJ's raft and then let JJ do the rest.

Having seen what happened to JJ, LB was acutely aware of the dangers circling his own raft. Dangers with long, sharp teeth and webbed claws patiently waiting to pounce if LB was careless enough to fall in, so he paddled vigorously to get back to the mainland.

Arriving safely at the beach he looked around to see if any other Avatar had spied him paddling towards the mainland. He didn't see any sign of danger lurking in the dense forest so continued to hide his raft. He might need this again at some time in the future.

Entity had other ideas about LB's future.

LB and Nun's Revenge (Nun) have become good friends since the start of the game. In the knowledge that they must, at some stage, meet as Avatars and try to eliminate each other, LB has tried to change the game rules and skew the game in his favour by becoming a 'friend' with Nun via the game's secure and secretive Avatar communication page.

He has persuaded Nun that when they meet, in the game, they should pair up to eliminate the other Avatars. That way only they would be left to share the winnings. They would, at some stage, agree who should throw the game to allow the other Avatar to win. A fifty-fifty split of the four million pound prize was well worth throwing the game at any of its levels, wasn't it? The owners of both Avatars saw this proposal as a good way to get rich, so they both agreed to the plan without revealing their real-life identities. One of them, however, was not participating in this agreement with the best of intentions…

*

Entity had covertly watched them communicate, so knew of their plan to change the rules.

It was annoyed by that, but it knew it couldn't do anything about it. Although Entity can engineer the rules to alter the players' life luck quota, it could not influence any of their thoughts.

*

Nun has just woken from a well-earned slumber. She had had a particularly difficult fight with Smelly Pants the previous evening and had slept a deep, restful sleep. She had eliminated Smelly Pants on the edge of a waterfall, pushing him over the edge of the precipice. Having peered into the precipice to make sure Smelly had been well and truly dispatched, Nun turned round and resumed her search for more Avatars in the forest. Her suit sensor had notified her of one about two miles from her present location. She had no idea who it was, but she was intent on turning the other Avatar's lights out for good. A share of that delicious four million pound prize would see her owner made for life.

Venturing out of her hide, Nun stretched the stiffness from her joints, had a good scratch and set about making some breakfast. Albeit bony, fried creature fish is tasty.

Breaking camp and eradicating any evidence that anyone had been there, Nun returned to the river to continue searching for Avatars to kill, hoping that she would meet up with LB before meeting any others. Two swords are better than one in this game.

Nun's thinking, at this point, was that a river always flows down to the sea. She would follow the path of the river in the hopes that the other Avatars had the same idea. With luck, she would happen across an unsuspecting Avatar and surprise it, unless, of course, the other Avatar happened across her first.

Along the way Nun came across a forest buggy. It was just sat there, powered down, resting on the ground and waiting to be found. These buggies are not the fastest or most comfortable of vehicles to travel on, but they are faster than walking, and riding would give Nun's suit a chance to fully recharge its strength. Another advantage of the forest buggies is that they are silent. They hover about eighteen inches above ground level, so they don't touch anything while they are in drive mode.

Furtively looking round, in case the bike's owner was watching, Nun looked over it for any damage or hidden IED's (Improvised Explosive Devices) but found none. The bike appeared to be in good condition and Nun wondered who, or why, it had been abandoned. '*Perhaps,*' Nun thought, '*it had once belonged to a living Avatar that had recently been eliminated. Ah, well. Never look a gift horse in the mouth.*' After mounting the bike and heading it in the direction of the river's flow she pressed down on the accelerator and shot off towards the sea.

She had travelled for about thirty minutes when her suit sensor flashed a warning. 'Danger! Opposing Avatar In range!' Slowing to a standstill, Nun had a decision to make. She could continue to search silently while riding the buggy. That would present a rather large target for any opposing Avatar. Or she could dismount and stand the risk of being heard while stalking through the undergrowth.

She decided that silence was the better choice to make.

*

Brushing the sandy beach with a small branch of leaves to hide his footprints, LB took one last look into the forest before heading inland. His thinking was that if any of the other Avatars were following the course of the river to the sea, he would see it first and hide from the opposing Avatar's approach in the hopes that he could surprise it.

Hours later, with the forest still silent, he decided to rest and have a meal. Sat on a tree stump, enjoying his meal of flame grilled creature meat, he was oblivious to Nun's presence because he had turned off his suit sensor for a bit of peace and quiet. He decided to have a short snooze after his meal, but he forgot to re-activate the suit sensor. It was a bad decision turning off his suit sensor. An even worse decision was not remembering to turn the sensor back on before having a nap. He laid down in the warm sunlight and soft grass, and shut his eyes.

He entered the room of dreams. Not so much a snooze, more of a fast asleep. His guard was down and with his suit sensor disabled he stood no chance of becoming alert to any danger whatsoever. His dream took him to a far-off place where everything was nice and warm and safe. If only he had remembered that *nothing* is safe in this forest, but his dream was far too interesting to leave.

*

Gliding silently through the forest, Nun allowed her concentration to lapse slightly.

In much the same way as a modern day driver disregards the road ahead while texting on his smart phone, Nun turned and looked backwards to see if she was being followed. Facing the front once more she was suddenly confronted by a tree branch reaching across the path. Unable to avoid it, Nun was knocked off the buggy and crashed heavily to the ground, making a lot of noise. The buggy carried on by itself for a good few yards, breaking branches and making more noise in the process.

Nun laid on the ground listening for anything that might have been attracted to the noise she had made. Nothing. With alert eyes she scanned the forest for movement. Nothing. She looked at the buggy, hovering in front of the tree it had run into, then made another detailed scan of the area. Still nothing. Fortunately, she had fallen onto a patch of turf and so was uninjured. The noise made retrieving the buggy and re-mounting it, however, was minimal but noticeable.

Continuing her journey, the buggy entered a clearing and Nun was suddenly alerted to a movement about twenty yards directly in front of her. LB had been woken by the noise of Nun's mishap and he emerged from the forest, head down, scratching his armpit and clearing a path for himself. He was oblivious to Nun's presence.

Nun had throttled back to a standstill and waited for the other Avatar to look up. LB stopped in his tracks when he saw Nun sat astride the buggy. He had not remembered to turn his suit sensor with its integral shield back on. The shield provided addition protection by diverting anything likely to penetrate his armour - spears, bullets and the like - and also gave LB additional strength.

"What's your name?" he shouted.

"Nun's Revenge. What's yours?"

"Lover Boy."

Nun breathed a sigh of relief when she heard LB call out his name.

"Are we still a team?" LB called out.

"I thought we were." Nun replied.

LB's plot to catch an Avatar off guard seemed, to him, to have worked but Nun was still suspicious of LB's motives. His antagonistic stance suggested something less than friendship.

"We are a team, aren't we?" probed Nun.

"Don't know, yet. That prize pot is worth having, isn't it?"

"Yeah, but we agreed to split it."

"Yeah. Well… I might have changed my mind."

"Oh, come on! Two million quid each is enough for both our owners to live on for ever. There's no need to be greedy, is there?"

"I guess you're right, but let's face it, four million quid is better than two, don't you think?"

Nun was flabbergasted. "We agreed, Lover Boy. We agreed to split the winnings. We agreed that as a team we would fare better than being alone. Why the sudden change of heart?"

"Haven't you heard? There's only four of us left. With you out of the way I can manage Sweetness and Black Hood on my own."

"I trusted you!"

"Shouldn't have…"

"You stinking, filthy, greedy pig!"

Nun reached for her gun but realised that it was absent. It had fallen out of its holster when she fell off the buggy.

"Oh dear. Lost your gun, have you?" laughed LB as he raised his own gun to fire.

In a flash, Nun thought *'Only one thing to do.'*

The buggy's throttle was opened to its full extent and it dashed forward in a flash.

Lover Boy aimed and squeezed his gun's trigger. The shot missed Nun by a fraction and the buggy was rapidly approaching him. He now realised what Nun's intention was. He quickly tried to re-load the gun but it was too late. The buggy crashed into his chest, propelling him upwards and backwards. His last thought was, 'S*hould have turned my shield back on...*'

The back of LB's head smashed onto a large boulder when he landed on his back. He flopped to the ground, lifeless, with blood staining the earth around his head. The back of his skull was badly fractured and had split open, spilling his brains over the base of the rock. There was no way he could have survived such a chest crushing impact from the buggy, or such a catastrophic blow to the head.

This Avatar's game was over…

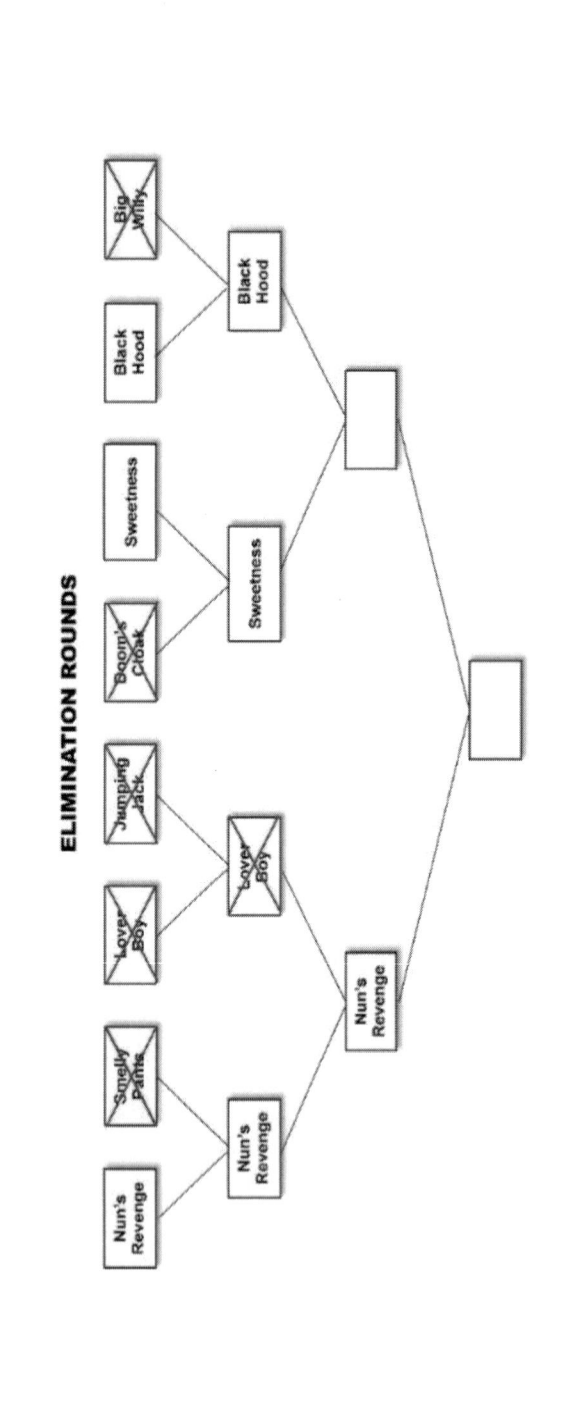

ELIMINATION ROUNDS

Round 1
- Big Willy vs Black Hood → **Black Hood**
- Sweetness vs Boom's Cloak → **Sweetness**
- Jumping Jack vs Lover Boy → **Lover Boy**
- Smelly Pants vs Nun's Revenge → **Nun's Revenge**

Round 2
- Black Hood vs Sweetness
- Lover Boy vs Nun's Revenge → **Nun's Revenge**

Final

DW entity smiled as it realised that the game rules were still intact.

*

William Arthur (Billy) lost his temper and threw his PC mouse across the room. He had just lost the chance of winning four million pounds by eliminating a load of dorks from the on-line game he had been playing. It had taken weeks of game-play to reach this level and he had been confident enough to win the game. Too confident, perhaps. He thought he had conned one of his opponents into thinking he was a good guy, and he had, but the other player recognised his strategy just before it was too late. In the very last second the other player was just a bit too quick for him and Billy was eliminated in a brutal way.

Billy's mistake was not checking that he had fully re-loaded his on-line Avatar's gun before setting it off on a trek to locate the other Avatars. The one and only bullet in his gun had missed his opponent by a fraction and he was mown down by a wretched forest buggy while trying to re-load. What an unexpected and, indeed, humiliating way to go.

Never mind. There may be another chance to win a prize such as this, some other day.

*

Billy was every inch the God's gift to women that he had portrayed to his friends and acquaintances from the time that he was at school. Most of the people that he knew thought he was an egotistical prat who loved himself more than anything, or anybody, else but they considered him harmless enough to be friends with him.

For some inexplicable reason he hadn't had any decent luck for years, in fact for most of his life- ever since he had caught measles while at school. His outward persona, however, had enabled him to have lots of affairs, usually with married women.

He homed in on married women for several reasons, and being a lorry driver afforded him many opportunities to meet his sexual conquests. Bars, dance halls, restaurants and hotels all had them. There were also many hitch-hikers willing to share his Yorkie Bar.

For a start, married women were more experienced than most single women. They knew their way around a man's body and so Billy didn't need to do much to enjoy his time with them.

Secondly, he was the proverbial single bloke. The catch that all women should have caught. This made him ultra attractive to married women and he knew that they would readily fall for his charms.

Thirdly, he knew that his liaisons with them would not become clingy. He ditched the clingy type after their first night together because he wanted to remain single, and clingy women have a habit of leaving their husbands for what they wrongly thought would be a long-lasting relationship. After all, Billy was not a marriage breaker, was he?

Next, an unwanted pregnancy would, most likely, be blamed on the husband unless, that is, the woman blabbed, or someone demanded a paternity test... but Billy would be long gone before any of that happened.

Fifth reason, by not having to worry about unwanted pregnancies he didn't need to spend time donning uncomfortable condoms before having sex.

This leads us to his sixth reason; married women were clean... he didn't have to worry about catching unwanted sexually transmitted diseases because married women just didn't have any to pass on, otherwise they wouldn't stay married, would they?

Finally, he knew that married women were discreet. At least, they were discreet enough not to let on to their husbands about the affair, but their discretion didn't always stretch to keeping quiet about it with their women friends. This was a good thing, from Billy's point of view. He had a reputation to keep, and he also had the strength to live up to that reputation... Up being the operative word, here, and he sometimes found several of the wife's friends ready to accommodate his desires...

Anyway, retrieving his PC mouse from where he had thrown it he replaced its battery and sat back at his desk, reflecting on his life to date.

He was now thirty-five years old. His run of bad luck started when he was a teenager.

He is the same God's gift now as he was back in his school days. Back then he hung out with two friends; a girl called Emma and his best friend at the time, Arthur Williams (Art). The boys' names were so much alike they hit it off as soon as they met in their first year at school. Emma joined them later.

In their final school year Emma had developed into a beautiful young woman and Billy couldn't wait to get into her pants. His shower exercise was always inspired by his fantasies about Emma, and what they would do together once Billy had found a way to get her on her own. Art, however, was always in the way so Billy never got the opportunity to persuade Emma to go for a walk somewhere private with him.

His bout of measles had given Art the chance to capture Emma for himself and Art and Emma had eventually married. At the time of Billy's measles incarceration Art and Emma's enhanced friendship angered Billy but he has since learned to live with his disappointment, and they remained friends. The three of them still meet up for frequent drinks, parties and BBQ's.

*

Okay. Right now, what Art didn't realise is that Billy and Emma had become more than good friends during the group's eighteen-year friendship.

Art's job as a surgeon kept him at the hospital long into the night, operating on somebody's brain tumour, or intercranial bleed caused by a fight with another drunken idiot, or a car crash. The operations he had to perform were complex, time consuming tasks that kept him away from Emma's bed, and Emma was now missing her bedtime cuddles… a lot.

Billy's charm had eventually appealed to Emma's desires and she succumbed to his smooth talk and persuasive manner. A "One last drink?" in front of Billy's TV one evening, led to a few hours of passion, and that affair had continued right up to today.

Billy thought his bad luck had eventually turned a corner for the better, and you would be forgiven if you thought that Entity had reset Billy's and Art's life's luck quota, but you would be wrong. Dark web Entity had other ideas in store for Billy.

Let's go back to Billy's schooldays, just for a second. Who was it that gave him the measles? Remember Mike? He who met Billy on his way back from seeing his Aunt May and offered to pass on his measles to Art but didn't. Well, Billy and Art and Emma all remained friends with Mike and they all occasionally met up for a drink.

One night, during a slack period in Art's busy schedule, Art and Mike met up for a drink. The conversation generally centred around work until Mike asked about Emma.

"How's Emma keeping? Still as beautiful as she ever was?"

"Yep. She's staying at her mum's house for a couple of days while her dad gets over a bout of pneumonia."

"Oh? I thought I saw her going into Billy's place on my way past. Maybe I was wrong."

"Yeah. Maybe. She phoned me earlier to let me know that she had arrived safely. What time did you think you saw her at Billy's?"

"Oh, right. Err, about seven p.m. I reckon it was some other woman. You know what Billy is like…"

"Yeah. Probably. Some other woman."

"The woman I saw is the spitting image of Emma, though. You don't reckon she's got a doppelganger, do you?"

They both laughed at that comment, but it didn't sit right with Art.

"I'll have to go, Art." Mike continued. "There's a good film on the telly that I want to watch."

With that, the men bid their goodbyes and Mike left Art to finish his drink.

Art sat and brooded about Mike's comment. Maybe Emma had called into Billy's place for something on her way to her mum's house, perhaps to let him know where she was going… Maybe. But why would she do that? She's never done that before, whenever she visited her mum. Maybe Mike had mis-recognised Emma for someone else… Maybe. Maybe she had popped in to return those books Art had borrowed. No, not that. Art remembered the books still sitting on the top of the sideboard when he left the house to meet Mike...

The drink was beginning to get the better of Art. Seven p.m. seemed a bit late for Emma to leave for her mum's place. If Mike was right about the time he saw her, and she had left Billy's house straight away, Emma wouldn't have got to her mum's place for a good fifteen minutes after she had phoned him to say that she had arrived. Was Mike right? Did he see Emma entering Billy's place?

If Mike was right, the implications were too much for Art to take in. He picked up his phone and looked at the time. Ten-thirty p.m. It was a bit late, but he phoned Emma's number. No reply, straight to voicemail. He then phoned Billy's number to see if Emma had called into his place before going on to Mum's place. No reply, also straight to voicemail.

Art had a choice to make. Put Mike's comment down to gossip and forget it, or call on Billy to ask if he had seen Emma that evening. His curiosity got the better of him and he opted for the latter choice.

Some five minutes later he pulled up in the street about four houses away from Billy's place - the only place left to park up. He was just about to get out of the car when he saw Emma through Billy's bedroom window, getting dressed… Billy really should close his bedroom curtains. Art decided to wait some more and after about five minutes he watched Emma exit through Billy's door, skip down the steps and head towards her own car, some thirty or so yards up the street.

'*What the hell…?*' thought Art. He was stunned to see Emma hurrying to her car. He then heard Billy calling to her.

"Emma. You've left your scarf."

Art watched as Billy chased after Emma who had stopped and turned to wait for Billy to catch up. Art pushed down on his brakes and put his electric car's engine into drive as he watched Emma and Billy kiss passionately in the middle of the street. It was now abundantly obvious what had been going on between them at this late hour.

Billy opened Emma's car door for her to get in. When the door closed the window was wound down and Art watched in anger as he saw Billy bend down for one last kiss goodnight. He shook with anger as he waited some more. His timing had to be right.

Emma drove off, not noticing Art's car parked close by.

Billy slowly walked down the middle of the road towards his house. He was too much into his thoughts of Emma laying on his bed to see Art's car speeding towards him. He looked up too late. Colliding with Art's car, he was flung into the air by the car's bonnet. He landed on his back, smashing his head onto the corner of the kerb stone.

Billy lay on the ground, lifeless, with blood staining the area around his head. The back of his skull was badly fractured and had split open, spilling his brains over the surrounding pavement. There was no way he could have survived such a chest crushing impact from Art's car, or such a catastrophic blow to the head.

Art didn't stop.

When he arrived home he carried on as if nothing had happened. He got a call from Emma's phone just as he was getting ready for bed.

"Hello, darling. You called me earlier," Emma chirped.

"Oh, yes." Replied Art. "I was just wondering how your dad was getting on with his meds."

"He's well on the way to recovering," she lied. She hadn't seen her dad yet because she was still driving to her mum's place.

"Okay. See you when you get back."

"Okay. Goodnight, darling."

*

Entity's influence was far reaching.

Art didn't mention that he'd seen Emma leave Billy's place until, weeks later, she came home and let Art know that she had just been to the Special Treatment Centre at the hospital and had been told by the doctor there that she had contracted Syphilis.

"Who from?" asked Art, quietly.

"Billy," replied Emma, looking away in embarrassment. Tears began to run down her cheeks.

"Oh? It must have been before he got run down by that hit-and-run driver… When you had forgotten your scarf."

"Yes, probably," declared Emma, head down in shame.

Her head suddenly snapped up to look Art in the face. "How did you know I'd forgotten my scarf?" she asked, eyes wide open, realising that Art must have seen her leave Billy's house that night and also realising what Art had done to Billy in a jealous rage.

Art sat back in his chair and calmly said, "That means you have passed the disease on to me."

"Yes," sobbed Emma, "but the doctor tells me it is treatable and with today's drugs we shouldn't have any lasting problems."

"I know that, Emma. Have you forgotten that I'm also a doctor? I've been having treatment for it for some time, now."

Emma didn't answer. She just sat and cried in the knowledge that Art's love for her was now gone. She also knew that the damage to their marriage that she had caused by being unfaithful to Art was irretrievable.

Art rose from his chair to go to bed. On the way to the door he turned and nonchalantly informed Emma that, "The spare room is made up. That's where you'll be sleeping from now on… I trusted you, Emma, but you betrayed that trust. You can continue to live here, if you want, but you must never, ever, let our children know what has happened between us."

Emma sat and cried long into the night, knowing that she and Art would never find the joys of marriage ever again.

*

What of Billy?

He died on the way to hospital. His head injury was too much for him to survive. The police never found out who the hit-and-run driver was. They assumed it was just another drunk driver and closed their file as a run of the mill unsolved road traffic accident.

William Arthur no longer exists in the real world. His luck had finally run out and he had died in much the same way that his Avatar in the game had died…

PLAYER STATUS

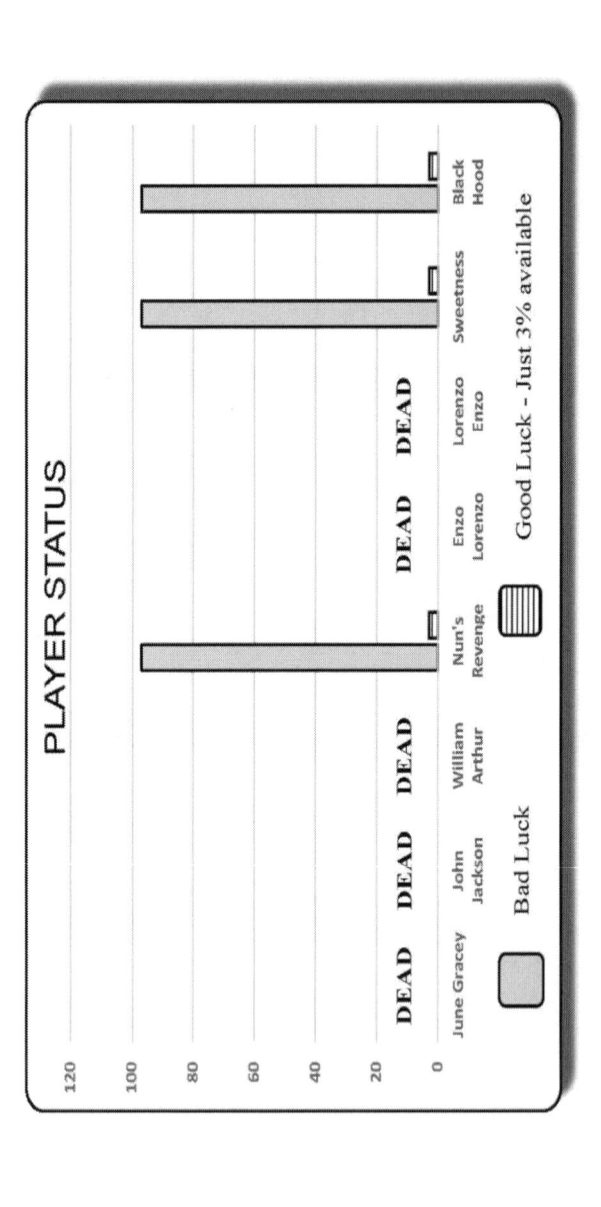

DEAD	DEAD	DEAD		DEAD	DEAD	
June Gracey	John Jackson	William Arthur	Nun's Revenge	Enzo Lorenzo	Lorenzo Enzo	Sweetness	Black Hood

Bad Luck Good Luck - Just 3% available

CHAPTER 20

Sweetness -v- Black Hood

Several weeks ago Sweetness had pulled a fast one on Doom's Cloak.

Pretending to be dead, she laid in a clearing on her stomach, eyes closed, lifeless, in the hopes that this pretence would lure out into the open an Avatar that was hiding in a cave. It worked. An easy kill, but not without its hazards.

The biggest problem she had, while playing dead, was the incessant biting of forest bugs and the burnt skin from the bugs' acid faeces. Deep pits would be left in her skin for some time to come, but the pain and suffering was worth it. By eliminating Doom's Cloak she had enabled her owner to progress to the next level in the game. Her owner had played the game for weeks and worked hard to get to this level, on some days long into the early hours. The big prize of four million pounds was now in sight and this Avatar's weary owner was beginning to think that the prize was his.

*

Sweetness had laid low in the cave that Doom's Cloak had used to hide from her.

She spent the weeks recuperating from the bug bites. Some of the bites had turned nasty and harboured infection, but Sweetness's medipak eventually cleared up the infections and she was now ready to venture out into the open, once more.

Doom's Cloak had left some useful tools in the cave for her to appropriate. There were knives, guns, battery packs, ammo and several medipaks. Of most use to Sweetness would have been the heavy jacket that deflected all sorts of projectiles. Unfortunately, the jacket was too small for her to wear. There was no way she would be able to zip up the front, and the sleeves only just covered her elbows. With some regret, she had to leave this in the cave. There was no point in lugging it around if it can't protect against the volley of missiles fired from an opposing Avatar's weapon.

She considered carrying the purloined rifle but she favoured light travel more than artillery and so left the rifle, and its ammo, in the cave after first rendering it harmless. Rifles are okay for long distance sniping but Sweetness placed a lot of faith in her trusty electric bolt gun. This had, after all, been instrumental in dispatching her opponent.

Eyes blinking against the bright sunlight, she cautiously peered out of the cave in case another Avatar fancied its chances against her. Nothing. The forest was as quiet as a church graveyard, so she took a few furtive steps into the open as a final test of her isolation. Still nothing. Breathing a sigh of relief she made her way into the darkness of the forest.

*

Black Hood (BH), you will recall, had managed to persuade Big Willy into thinking he had walked away from a stand-off between them. He had enticed Big Willy out of his cave after putting him under siege for a couple of weeks and Big Willy had been poisoned by BH's doctored stew.

As he silently made his way through the forest, BH noticed that more sunlight was beginning to shine through the tree canopies. It was apparent that the denseness of the forest was beginning to thin out and he perceived that he was approaching its perimeter. He wondered what surprises lay ahead of him.

On reaching the forest's boundary he looked out over a valley of lush greenery, intersected by paths that led to a small hamlet. It was clear that the hamlet had been abandoned many years earlier. Some of the buildings had been torched and there was no indication that anyone had occupied any of the remaining buildings for quite some time. Perhaps there had been a raid on the settlement by some marauding Avatars? Maybe the occupants had been attacked by a pack of creatures? Who knows? None of this mattered to BH. His thoughts were on looting what he could recover from the abandoned buildings.

It was now mid-day and he thought that perhaps one of the buildings was in a sufficiently good condition for him to rest up for the night. He made his way down the valley slope, cautiously looking round to make sure that he was not being stalked.

*

On the opposite side of the valley, Sweetness also appeared from the edge of a forest that cloaked the top of that hillside.

The sun was beginning to set so instead of exploring the little hamlet that she spied on, from behind a convenient boulder, she decided to wait until the following day to descend the valley slope. BH had entered the village hours before so Sweetness didn't know he was residing in one of the abandoned buildings. She returned deep into the forest to start a campfire and roast some creature meat that she had caught earlier in the day.

After a restless night of swatting bugs that had fancied a tasty meal of Avatar flesh, she poked the embers of her fire into life and roasted the remains of her creature meat for breakfast. Washing down her meal with cool water from a nearby stream, she put out the fire and obliterated any signs that she had been in the vicinity.

Making her way to the edge of the forest, once more, her thoughts were on what she would do with her winnings, if she was lucky enough to win the game.

*

Entity kept watch on Sweetness with some suspicion. He didn't want any more curved balls thrown in his direction...

Lorenzo Enzo had, Entity recalled, chucked a curved ball at its systems and this had forced his terminals into the blue screen mode. It had taken Entity quite some time to regain control of its systems, and it was desperate to prevent that happening again.

Never again...

*

Unlike Sweetness, BH had had a peaceful and restful night's sleep. He awoke with enthusiasm, arrogantly thinking that nothing would now stand in his owner's way of winning the big prize.

Entity, incidentally, was watching BH, also. With a quota of just three percent good luck available to the players, knew that at least one of them was destined to perish shortly.

BH had found some tins of food in one of the cupboards in the kitchen of the building he had slept in. He lit a fire in the hearth and cooked the remains of his creature meat, loading his breakfast plate with roast meat and tinned veg.

He had a feeling that today was going to be a lucky day. A day, he thought, when he would dispatch one of the few Avatars standing in his owner's way to that four million pound prize.

*

From Sweetness's commanding position behind the boulder she spied on the hamlet and was surprised to see smoke rising from one of its chimneys.

It is clear that the hamlet was not as abandoned as she thought it had been last evening. Was there an opposing Avatar in the building, or was there a remnant occupier, stoic enough to have fought off any attack that rendered the rest of the hamlet unsafe to live in? Going down to the settlement was a gamble. There could be several Avatars lying in wait. She doubted, however, that there were many creatures down there. Creatures and settlements don't mix well, and settlers were usually the ones to come out on top in a settler/creature contest.

She made up her mind that only one being was down there. Either an opposing Avatar or a surviving resident. If it was a resident… no problem. If it was an Avatar she would have to fight, as much as she hated to fight. She slowly made her way down the slope towards the hamlet.

*

BH hummed a tune to himself as he washed up his breakfast things. He suddenly froze in front of the kitchen window. He saw another Avatar making its way down the lower slope of the valley towards the hamlet. It would be in the street within minutes.

Common sense told him that he should hide up somewhere and try to ambush the approaching Avatar, but what's the point? That Avatar would have seen smoke rising from the cottage chimney and it would now know that somebody was in residence. The other Avatar could sneak in and out of the buildings and there was a fifty-fifty chance that BH could be ambushed himself.

No, his best chance, he thought, was to meet the other Avatar out in the open and have a shoot-out where he could see what he was aiming at. That, in itself, was a gamble, but a gamble worth taking. After all, his owner's shooting skills had improved massively since the start of the game and BH was confident that he could out-draw any of his opponents.

He quickly donned his small arms holster, checked that his gun was fully loaded with bullets, took a deep breath and slowly walked to the cottage door.

*

By the time BH had prepared for his gunfight, Sweetness had arrived at the end of the street.

"I know you're in there." she called. "Come out and show yourself."

She slowly walked up the centre of the street, her hand resting on the handle of her electric bolt gun. When she reached the middle of the street, about three or four doors from the smoking chimney cottage, she stopped to see what would happen. Nothing.

'Has he gone out the back door to ambush me?' she thought.

Her eyes oscillated from side to front, seeking any movement that would give her opponent's Avatar's position away. Still nothing. Perhaps a bit of encouragement would work.

"What's wrong? Scared of a trivial little female Avatar, are we? Not good enough to face me?"

The goading worked. BH flung the cottage door open and walked into the centre of the street, his hand resting on his gun. In a classic western style shoot-out, the Avatars faced each other. Sweetness faced BH with eyes of steel, but BH had to squint against the rising sun. He had been unfortunate enough to walk into the street with the sun shining directly in his eyes.

"What's your name?" asked BH.

"Sweetness," she answered. "What's yours?"

"Sweetness, eh? I've heard about you. Some reckon you're good with that electric bolt gun."

The sun slowly ascended over the horizon. BH peered at Sweetness through half closed eyes.

"Too good for your archaic weapon." Sweetness replied. "Don't you know that electric bolts travel at light speed. Your little toy won't even send a bullet out of its chamber before you feel the might of a lightning bolt," she sneered.

BH waited. The moment had to be just right. With his left hand he fiddled with his belt buckle until he saw a reflection from the sun bounce off it onto Sweetness's legs. He had to buy just a few more seconds before he could make a move.

"Do you fancy pairing up with me as a team? Two guns are better than one."

Sweetness thought about that suggestion, then replied, "Nah. I've heard about Lover Boy's plan to hook up with someone. That didn't end well."

'Just a couple more seconds…' thought BH.

"You sure it's fully charged?" he asked. "The last thing you need right now is a dim light coming from it."

"I'm not stupid. I charged it overnight, while you slept. Do you want some time to pray?"

"No, I'll be the one praying…"

Now was the time to move. BH tilted his belt buckle to reflect the sun's full glare into Sweetness's eyes. Her concentration was broken, just for a second, as the reflection from BH's belt buckle made her blink, wrecking any chance of her seeing where she was aiming. She quickly drew her gun and fired bolt after bolt at nothing important. BH had seen his opportunity, dropped to his knee and drew his own gun out of its holster in unison with Sweetness, but through slitted eyes *he* could see where he was aiming. Two, three, four bullets were propelled from his gun and all hit their target.

Sweetness was dead before she hit the ground.

This Avatar's game was over…

ELIMINATION ROUNDS

- Nun's Revenge
  - Nun's Revenge
    - Smelly Dame
  - Nun's Revenge
    - Lover Boy
      - Lover Boy
      - Jumping Jack
- Black Hood
  - Sweetness
    - Sweetness
    - Doom's Cloak
  - Black Hood
    - Black Hood
    - Big Willy

Jack Johnson has reached rock bottom. He is just about as low in the pecking order of life as one can get. The lowest of the low.

Jack, you will recall, was a tech entrepreneur who was at the top of both his trade and his social media pages. Unfortunately, he and his trusted Finance Director had both made some dubious investments and they lost all their firm's financial assets in the process. To add insult to injury, he had lost his home, his wife, his children, his social standing and, above all else, his self-respect.

All this was due to the fact that his quota of good luck had run out and this now lounged at zero - totally depleted. All Jack had to look forward to from the time his life's luck quota had been reset by Entity were lashings of bad luck… And boy, did he have a lot of bad luck!

Entity congratulated itself on its excellent work… A job well done.

*

It has now been a couple of years since Jack's business had folded.

After losing his home, and his family, he became the proverbial bum, living off the streets and surviving by hanging around the restaurant bins for scraps of unwanted food. His hair is matted, he is emaciated, his once pearly-white teeth now resemble a chequerboard, and his clothes have clearly been passed around a few other homeless men. He acquired his top coat, for example, by stripping it from a dead bum he found lying in some alley.

Jack has just one friend in this world of dossing around and begging for pennies. That friend is Peregrine Forbes-Miller, his ex-Finance Director. Peregrine is now the assistant manager of an internet cafe. Despite his eminent qualifications, that job was the only one he could get after Jack's business crashed. The reputation for being a Finance Director that makes poor investment calls, it seems, resounds loudly in the world of company accounting... Or maybe his quota of good luck had been depleted? Only Entity can answer that.

Anyway, Peregrine can't shake the thought that he had had a hand in the collapse of Jack's business, notwithstanding the fact that Jack, himself, shared much of the guilt. Jack calls into the internet cafe most days and sits in one of the isolated booths, the one in the darkest corner of the shop, to drink some of Peregrine's coffee and play the game - that game - the one where the winner will net a huge win of four million pounds. He sits in this dark corner courtesy of Peregrine, who never charges Jack for his internet time.

Unfortunately, Jack's female Avatar in that game has just been eliminated, so the prospects of escalating Jack's prospects to a better life have now been well and truly squashed.

Jack sat back in his chair and sobbed into his hands, his tears of hopelessness running down his cheeks and falling into his lap. He just could not understand how the hell he had got into this deep, dark void, with no idea of how to get out of it. The game, as far as he was concerned, was his last, and only, chance to redeem his self-respect.

Peregrine came and sat next to him.

"Lost the game?" he asked.

"Yeah. Now I've really got nothing. Nowhere else to go." grumbled Jack.

"Don't say that, Jack. Do you want to come over to my place later? You can have a shower, a decent meal, and you can crash on my settee for a while."

"Nah. That's not fair to you, and anyway, I doubt your wife will take kindly to me stinking the place out with these filthy rags."

"Don't worry about that. Just come and get a decent night's sleep, for once."

"Thanks, Peregrine, but no thanks. You know what? If I had a gun I'd top myself. What else have I got to look forward to?"

"Aw, come on, Jack. Nothing is as bad as that. You're just going through a bad patch. It'll get better, I'm sure."

"No chance," replied Jack, "I'm resigned to a life of begging, rummaging in dustbins and stealing to survive."

'*Stealing,*' thought Peregrine. '*Now there's an idea...*'

"Jack, come back here at closing time tonight. I might have an idea. I've certainly got something to give to you."

"What?"

"Come back later. You'll see."

Jack left the internet cafe and parked himself across the street in a derelict shop's recessed entrance doorway. He didn't have anything else to do or anywhere else to go, so he thought that he may as well sit there for the rest of the day. When he saw all the punters leaving the internet cafe he stood up and walked across the road. He was met by Peregrine.

Peregrine looked up and down the street to see if anyone was watching, and he then beckoned Jack inside.

"Come in, quick. I've got to lock up."

Jack entered the cafe and stood in the middle of the room, waiting for Peregrine to make the cafe door secure. Peregrine then ushered Jack into the office at the back of the shop.

"Sit down while I make you a cup of coffee." Peregrine pointed to a chair and disappeared into the kitchen to make the coffee. Returning with two mugs, a few minutes later, he put Jack's coffee on the low table in front of the visitor's chairs and sat opposite him.

Jack started the conversation. "What is this idea you mentioned earlier?"

"Oh," replied Peregrine, "Just let me get something for you, first."

Peregrine stood and walked over to the manager's desk. He took out something wrapped in a tea-towel sized cloth and sat down opposite Jack once more.

"Do you know that on most days this place takes about two thousand pounds from the punters? Now, today is Monday, so by Saturday there is about ten thousand pounds in this drawer," pointing to the desk drawer. "The manager's a clown. I've told him time and time again to get a decent safe, but he just ignores me."

"So?" questioned Jack, with a hint of suspicion.

"So, what if we were to get robbed at, say, closing time on Saturday?"

Jack stared at Peregrine for a long few minutes. With a furrowed brow, he eventually asked, "So… What's that got to do with me?"

Peregrine unfolded the article that had patiently sat in his lap to reveal the handgun that the cafe's owner kept to chase off any would-be robbers.

Jack stared at it, Peregrine's words bouncing around the inside of his head.

"Are you out of your head? I can't do it, Peregrine. People know that you let me use the PC's for free. They'll know it was an inside job."

"No, no they won't. It's so easy, Jack. You come here just after closing time on Saturday. Nobody will be here. I'll be locking up and you barge your way in. Find a hoody from somewhere and wear it with the hood up. Keep your head down so the shop's camera won't see your face, wave the gun around and make me come to the office door. After you've kicked the door in make me get inside. After I've emptied the drawer, you whack me in the face and leave by the back door. I'll wait for you to get clear, then stumble back into the shop and telephone the cops. Who's to know it was you, as long as you don't show your face to the camera? Dump the gun somewhere far away and you're home and dry, with ten thousand quid to help you buy some fresh clothes."

Jack thought long and hard about the plan.

"Can't do it," said Jack. "If I get caught, I get life in prison for armed robbery."

"You can do it, Jack. What have you got to lose? At least, in prison you'll be able to shower, and have a warm bed to sleep in, with three meals a day. Even that is an improvement on what you've got right now!" declared Peregrine.

Once more, Jack thought long and hard. Peregrine was right. What did Jack have to lose? Absolutely nothing, because he's already got nothing. He took the gun out of Peregrine's hand.

"How are you going to account for the missing gun?"

"I don't have to. The manager, normally locks this office so I can't use it. He forgot, tonight. He won't say a word about the gun 'cos it's unlicensed and he'll be in for some jail time if he does mention it. I drop the night's takings through the letter box," pointing to the letter box in the office door, "and he arrives in the morning and drops the takings into the drawer. The stupid prat doesn't even lock the drawer. On Sunday, he carries the takings to the bank and puts it in their drop box with his deposit slip."

Jack stared at the gun, torn between going along with the plan or staying on the straight and level path.

"Take the gun, Jack. It's not loaded, so you can't do any damage with it."

Jack put the gun into his pocket.

Neither Jack nor Peregrine knew that their conversation had been recorded by the camera and microphone, hidden in the office's dummy smoke alarm.

On Tuesday morning the internet cafe's manager was seen entering the police station...

*

Jack mulled over the plan for the rest of the week.

What could go wrong? Nobody knew or even recognised him. He could hide the gun for future use, even go back the following week to double his own takings. The money would certainly make life for him a lot easier. He might even be able to get his family back if they could see that he had improved his lot.

Saturday arrived, and Jack visited the internet cafe at his usual time. Peregrine saw him enter the shop and gave Jack the thumbs up with raised eyebrows to question if the plan was on. Jack returned the thumbs up.

After using one of the shop's PC's, Jack went across the road and again sat in the opposite shop's recessed doorway until he saw the punters leaving the cafe at closing time. With some trepidation he crossed the road and entered the cafe.

He didn't see the plain clothes policeman, hiding in a similar doorway recess five or six doors down, radio his colleagues waiting in their vans and cars parked round the corner. They all took up position quietly at the front of the shop and in the rear alleyway after Jack had entered the cafe. No sirens. No car horns. No lights. Nothing to indicate their presence, and the cafe was surrounded.

As soon as the door to the cafe closed behind Jack he waved his gun around for the benefit of the shop camera and then roughly manhandled Peregrine to the office door. Pushing him into the office after kicking the door in, the two men looked at each other, both breathing heavily, adrenalin coursing through their veins. Inside the office, and away from the shop camera, Peregrine handed Jack the shopping bag containing the week's takings.

"Shut your eyes," suggested Jack as he balled his fist and took aim at Peregrine's face.

Peregrine closed his eyes and steeled himself against Jacks punch. Jack didn't just throw one punch, he planted several on Peregrine's face to make a good job. Peregrine dropped to the floor in a semi-conscious state.

Wrapping the shopping bag full of money into a roll he put the gun in his pocket and made for the rear door. As soon as he opened it he was faced with a barrier of armed police, all pointing their guns and rifles at Jack.

"Drop the bag and lie on your face," he was ordered.

Jack turned to dive back into the shop, but realised that several armed policemen had entered the shop through the front door. A couple of them were kneeling on Peregrine's back, fitting him with the mandatary bracelets. Jack stood there for a few seconds trying to take in what he could see, his head oscillating from front to rear. He knew there was no way out for him, now, and he had a difficult decision to make. He dropped the bag onto the floor and slowly reached into his pocket.

"Lie down on your front with your hands behind your back! I won't say this again."

Revealing the gun, Jack thought to himself, *'There's no way that I'm going to prison.'*

"Put the gun down and lie on your front. Last chance…"

Jack slowly raised the empty gun and pointed it towards the row of officers. Not two, not three, not four bullets were fired. Twenty bullets all hit their target.

Entity was, again, pleased with its day's work.

Jack Johnson no longer exists in the real world. His luck had finally run out and he had died in much the same way as his Avatar had died…

PLAYER STATUS

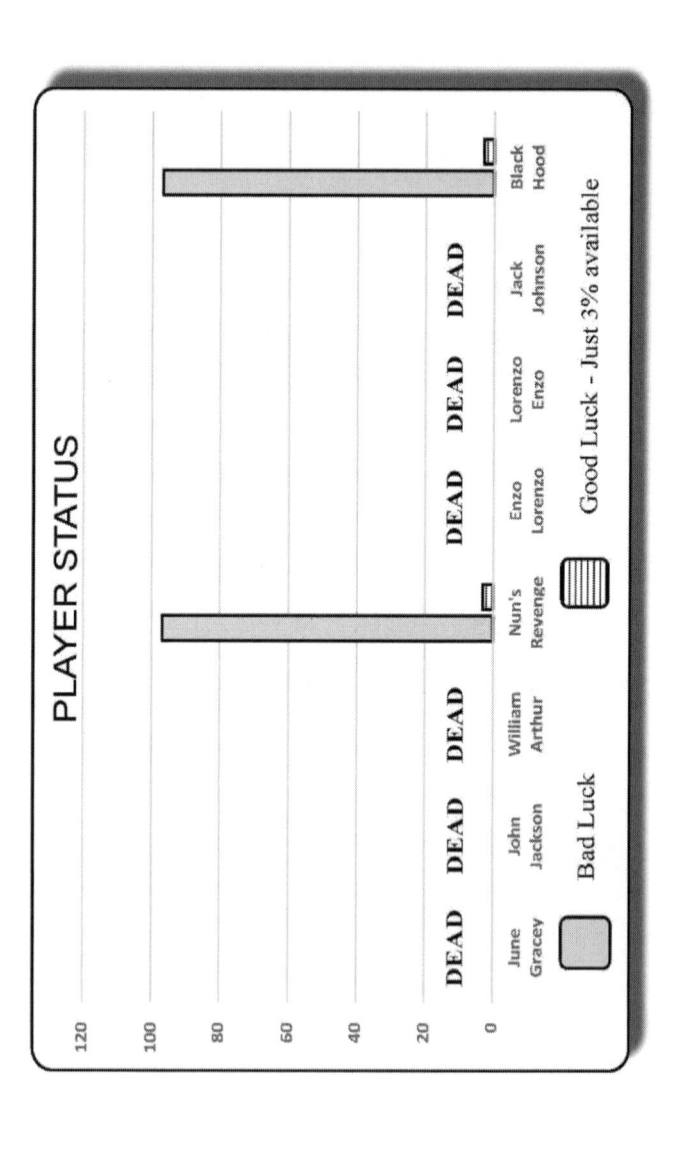

DEAD	DEAD	DEAD		DEAD	DEAD	DEAD	
June Gracey	John Jackson	William Arthur	Nun's Revenge	Enzo Lorenzo	Lorenzo Enzo	Jack Johnson	Black Hood

Bad Luck

Good Luck - Just 3% available

CHAPTER 21

The Final Round

Nun's Revenge -v- Black Hood

The final round. The last push. The end game. Call it what you will, but six Avatars have now been eliminated from the game, leaving just two to battle it out.

Entity is pleased, so far, with the expeditious way in which the Avatars and their owners have been dispatched. It is, however, intent on making sure that none of the remaining players will be around to collect that big prize. Not one!

The smell of money has grown stronger for all players at each level of the game, but the final two players have had to work long and hard to reach the level of competency required to win this game. Today, another Avatar will be eliminated. Neither of the two remaining game players know it, yet, but the life of that Avatar's owner will also be extinguished.

*

A few days ago, Nun's Revenge (Nun) dispatched Lover Boy (LB). Nun had thought that she and LB had paired up to work as a team but LB had deceived her. Nun had to think quickly to turn the tables on LB.

She has reached the final level in the game and she now has just one more Avatar to kill - Black Hood.

The journey to this level has been hard for Nun. At the start of the game the elimination rounds were easy. Lots of wannabe winners were eliminated from the game with ease. However, progress to this level got markedly harder when she reached the final three elimination rounds. What her owner didn't know was that the dark web entity had taken over running of the game and, indeed, the game players' luck quota, and six of them had died in a similar way to that of their Avatars. It's tough at the top.

Anyway, Nun sat quietly reflecting on her progress while resting on a tree stump. Her owner also sat back and reflected on the Avatar's successes.

Nun took stock of her weapons. She had a forest buggy - not much use as a weapon unless she could run her opponent over, like she did with LB, but that required a run-up to gather the necessary speed to do some damage. She was sure that BH was too savvy to let her do that.

She had been relatively lucky dispatching Smelly Pants. After a fight with him she pushed Smelly over a ravine and the fall onto rocks below killed him.

She had acquired several small arms from the Avatars that she had killed in the early stages of the game; knives, a muscle nullifying lasso, some unconscious spray, some ultrasonic Avatar repellent, knuckle dusters, a telescopic baseball bat and a some nunchucks. She also owned a magic sword that she had taken from Smelly's dead body. Nothing for long range attacks - all her armoury was designed for close contact combat so she would need to get BH close up to eliminate him, but after her scuffle with Smelly she didn't fancy another brawl.

She thought that perhaps she could rig something up for BH to walk into. Maybe a spike lined pit, or swinging log, or a leg trap, but these required time to construct and she knew that time was something she didn't have.

She was right about the time aspect.

BH had acquired an Avatar suit sensor on his travels and had been tracking Nun for several days. She knew this, but she also knew that she didn't have much of a defence system to rely on.

BH had approached to within a few hundred yards of Nun, so his sensor display was showing a strong signal. Unfortunately, a suit sensor was not something that Nun had had the opportunity to acquire.

As Nun rested she heard the rustle of foliage to her left. Listening, attentively, things seemed to be all quiet. Nothing there, but it is worth taking a better look from on high. She quickly climbed the nearest tree to perch on one of its branches. Looking out towards the rustling noise she had heard, she saw BH heading in her direction, rifle at the ready. With no long range weapon she knew that her weapons would be no match for BH's rifle, but she didn't have any plan ready to overcome BH.

BH had also been keeping his eyes peeled and he saw Nun climb the tree. When she perched on the branch and looked in his direction he froze, but it was too late. She had seen him. He raised his rifle and fired. The bullet narrowly missed Nun, but she felt its disturbed airstream as it passed by.

'*Too close for comfort,*' she thought and quickly shimmied down the tree to make for her forest buggy.

BH fired off another two shots. This time one of the bullets cut a groove in Nun's thigh. The other bounced off the buggy's engine. Nun winced in pain but ignored the wound and ran for the buggy. Mounting it, she shot off into the darkness of the forest. BH cursed his hurried aim. If he had had just one second more time he might have aimed better and released a bullet that would have hit Nun where it really hurt.

BH continued to track Nun through the forest. Nun thought she had out-manoeuvred him, but Entity had a few tricks up its sleeve. The first thing Nun noticed as she dashed through the forest was that the buggy's engine began to stutter and lose power. As the buggy slowed, Nun looked down at her thigh to see blood oozing through her trouser leg. She put the buggy into auto-steer, took out her handkerchief and tied it round her leg to stem the flow of blood.

The problem with auto-steer is that it slows the machine to compensate for obstructions that it detects in its trajectory. This allowed BH to make up some ground between Nun and himself.

The engine stutter, Nun knew, had to be corrected. Until that was fixed she couldn't release the buggy from auto-steer.

Bending down to see what the problem was, she saw that one of BH's bullets had clipped a wire when it ricocheted off the engine. Using her multi-purpose knife Nun cut the wire, which caused the buggy to stop. As the buggy slowed to a standstill Nun stripped off some covering from both of the cut ends and then quickly twisted the bare ends of the wire together. The buggy's display lit up as new life coursed through the repaired wire from its battery. With a sigh of relief, Nun straightened up to disengage auto-steer and put the engine into manual drive. A cursory glance over her shoulder confirmed that BH was closing in on her.

BH had made up a lot of the ground between him and Nun during the buggy's stand down and he was now about twenty yards away from Nun. He had seen Nun bent over the engine but rather than fire off another hurried shot he decided to keep running in the hopes that Nun was unable to repair the buggy. The buggy suddenly dashed off again before he could get any closer.

The wound on Nun's leg had opened up again and blood began to flow through her tunic. She bent down to reposition the handkerchief while the buggy rocketed through the forest.

Having repositioned her hanky, Nun sat up to re-focus on her line of travel and was immediately confronted by a massive tree trunk standing proudly in the way. The buggy's speed was too fast for Nun to avoid the tree and it smashed into the tree's trunk. Nun was thrown forward. Her shoulder clipped the tree trunk and she landed heavily three or four metres away.

Nun lay on her back, dazed and semi-conscious. BH saw this and hurried to catch Nun unawares. As Nun sat up and shook the fog from her head BH ran up to her and drew out his sheath knife. A rifle wasn't any good at close range, so he thought he could dispatch Nun quickly with the knife. Nun saw his approach and quickly pulled herself up into a kneeling position. She drew her magic sword from its scabbard. Too late. BH had managed to get close enough for him to kick the sword out of Nun's hand.

The fight between the two remaining Avatars was long and hard. It was violent and bloody, but only one of them could survive to win the prize pot. Both Avatars had had their weapons knocked from their hands during the conflict and both Avatars continually tried to reach them, frustratingly laying on the ground just out of reach. Tiredness began to entice the Avatars to make costly mistakes and they both now carried the scars of their fight. Battered, bloody and bruised the Avatars continued to roll around on the ground, throwing punches and attempting wrestling moves to get into a position convenient enough to reach for one of the weapons. Eventually, one of them was able to dodge away from the other. Rolling towards the weapons the Avatar took hold of the knife.

Deftly avoiding Nun's attempt at a punch, BH drove his knife into Nun's chest. He then watched as Nun's life ebbed away from her.

This Avatar's game was over…

ELIMINATION ROUNDS

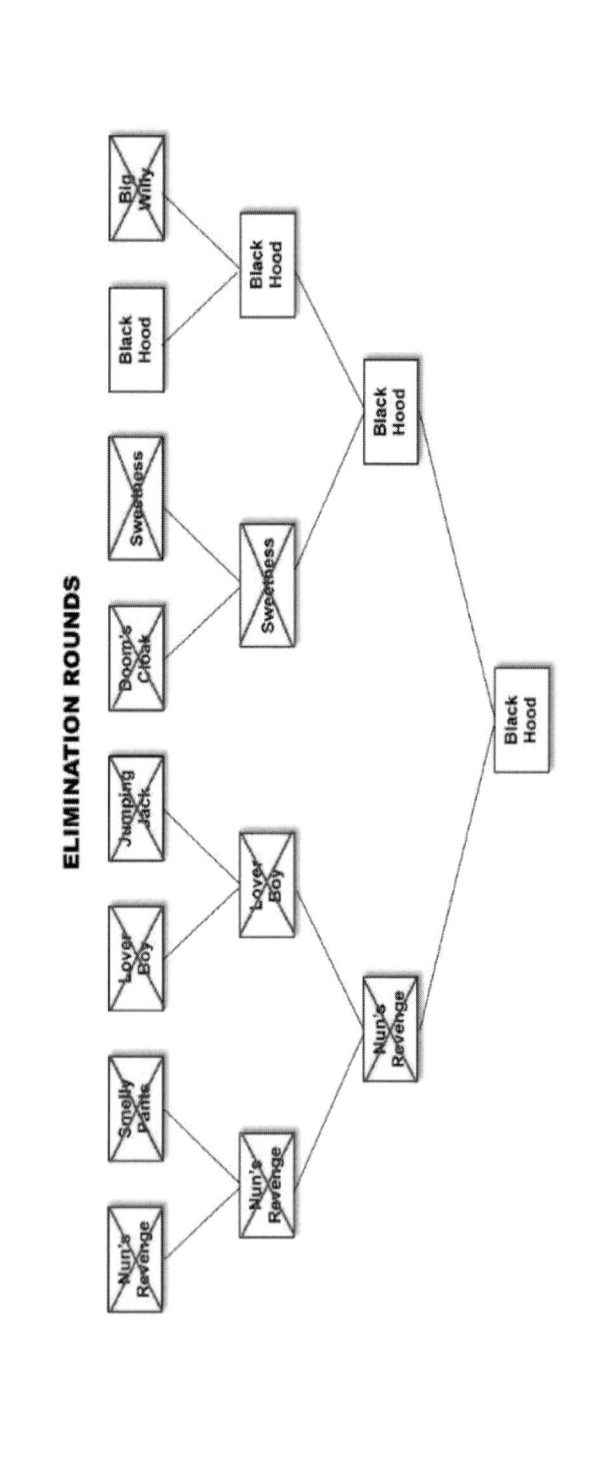

- Big Willy ─┐
            ├─ Black Hood ─┐
- Black Hood ┘   │
                            ├─ Black Hood ─┐
- Sweetness ─┐   │   │
            ├─ Sweetness ──┘   │
- Doom's Cloak ┘   │
                                           ├─ Black Hood
- Jumping Jack ─┐   │
               ├─ Lover Boy ─┐   │
- Lover Boy ────┘   │   │
                             ├─ Nun's Revenge ┘
- Smelly Pants ─┐   │
               ├─ Nun's Revenge ┘
- Nun's Revenge ┘

In fact, the game was over for everyone.

Black Hood is now the last Avatar standing.

Sister Gracey June breathed a sigh of relief, in the knowledge that a four million pound pot of money was there for the taking. It had been hard work, but it was well worth it.

*

Arthur Williams (Art) sat back and deliberated over his game.

'*What should I have done to avoid such a conflict,*' he thought. '*Ah well. perhaps I'll get another chance, one day,*' he sighed, putting down his gaming handset and standing up to stretch the tiredness from his aching neck.

Noticing the time, he remembered that he had an important operation to supervise the following day, so he made his way to his bed. Calling into the bathroom from his den he disturbed Emma.

Emma, you will recall, was relegated to the spare bedroom by Art after he found out that she had been having an affair with his long time friend Billy. She had passed a venereal infection on to him that she had caught from Billy.

Art had run Billy down with his car in a jealous rage and killed Billy for betraying their friendship, and Emma knew he had murdered her lover and had got away with it. She was given a choice by Art - get out of the marital home or continue to live there, relegated to the spare room. Art's thinking was that they could share the house, but not the marriage.

Emma should have reported Art to the police, but she knew that she had no evidence to prove her allegation of murder. Anyway, she now hated Art for depriving her of her lover. She detested him, loathed him, wanted him dead... And revenge is best served cold.

After Billy's death, as the days grew to weeks, her loathing for Art festered away until she could stand it no longer.

'Why should he sit in his den, playing computer games and enjoying himself, while I have to live this lonely life of contempt from him?' she thought. *'What can I do to be rid of him?'*

Without realising it, Emma's dark thoughts were being managed and manipulated by Entity!

Having retired to bed Art fluffed up his pillow, settled down and closed his eyes.

His thoughts turned to what he *could* have achieved if he had won that four million pound pot. He could have bought Emma a house to move into so that he could better enjoy his freedom from her. He could plough some money into research, or sponsor a medical student, or just buy a boat and sail off into the blue skies, leaving all his troubles and woes behind him. It wasn't long before he was fast asleep.

Emma entered his bedroom holding a kitchen knife that she had secreted away hours earlier. She stood for a moment, reflecting on the good times she had had with Art

- their marriage, their children - but nothing would compensate for the way Art had murdered Billy, and the way in which he had treated her since committing that crime.

She sat on the edge of his bed, bent and whispered in his ear. "Art, Wake up."

Art stirred and Emma whispered some more. "Art, it's Emma. Wake up. Open your eyes and look at me."

PLAYER STATUS

							WINNER
1							
0.9							
0.8							
0.7							
0.6							
0.5							
0.4							
0.3							
0.2							
0.1	DEAD	DEAD	DEAD	DEAD	DEAD	DEAD	
0	June Gracey	John Jackson	William Arthur	Arthur Williams	Enzo Lorenzo	Lorenzo Enzo	Jack Johnson	Sister Gracey

Art slowly opened his eyes and looked up to see Emma's face close to his. "What do you want?" he asked.

Emma kissed him on the lips, a soft, long and passionate kiss. She then stood and, to Art's horror, plunged the knife into his chest. She watched, coldly and dispassionately, as Art's life ebbed away from him.

Arthur Williams no longer exists in the real world. His luck had finaly run out and he had died in much the same way as his Avatar had died…

*

Entity hadn't yet finished with Emma. It had, of course, engineered a way for Art to discover her infidelity with Billy, but there was still a loose end to Art and Emma's story - did Emma get away with murder?

In short, the answer is no.

As Art's life force left his body Emma dropped the knife to the floor and went to the bathroom to wash the blood from her hands. She had no feelings for Art's demise. In fact, she had no feelings at all. She just stood in front of the basin looking down at her hands while she washed them, totally devoid of any feelings whatsoever. In a trance-like state she dried her hands and went downstairs to sit quietly on the settee and gaze into space.

A couple of hours later there was a knock on the door to the house, which was ignored. Another knock, again ignored. Emma's daughter, Rose, walked round to the back of the house to see if the kitchen door was accessible. She knew that Emma was at home because she had phoned earlier and had spoken to her. Emma had confirmed that she would stay in until Rose arrived to have a cup of tea and a chat.

Rose opened the kitchen door and poked her head inside.

"Mum? It's Rose. Are you there?"

No response.

"Mum?" a little louder.

'*Why is she not answering?*' thought Rose.

Mystified, Rose stepped into the kitchen and walked towards the lounge, calling her mum on the way. Reaching the door to the lounge she saw the top of Emma's head resting against the back of the settee.

'*Ah, she's asleep.*' thought Rose, going to the front of the settee to gently shake Emma to awaken her.

"Wake up, mum. It's only me."

Still no response.

Rose gave Emma another shake, this time a little harder, but Emma's head just lolled forward onto her chest. Rose gently lifted it, at the same time calling to Emma. Rose's hand suddenly let go of Emma's chin when she felt her cold, lifeless skin.

"Mum? What's wrong?" panicked Rose.

She again shook her, this time more violently than the other times, repeatedly calling to her. Emma's body slouched sideways and lay on the settee, lifeless. Rose stood and looked down in horror as she watched the empty pill bottle fall out of Emma's hand and drop to the floor.

Emma will now join Art, and the rest of the dead game players lounging in Entity's really warm clubhouse, to be abused, berated and ill-treated for the rest of eternity.

Dark web Entity was pleased with that day's work…

CHAPTER 22

A Contract

Four years ago David Smithers sat in an office, typed away on a company keyboard and answered people's stupid questions that had been dialled into an internet help line. He was a techie, an internet help line techie to be precise, and he was bored.

He was weary of the public's inane, ridiculous questions about how to turn on their PC, or "Why has my screen turned blue?" or "Where have all my apps gone?"

'*Why don't these people simply learn to use this stuff properly?*' he asked himself. '*If only they would go on a course, or something, my job might be a bit less boring. I might even get some interesting questions.*'

Day in, day out, Dave sat there waiting for the phone to ring. He read the morning's paper, he did the crossword, he manicured his nails, he drew pictures, he gawked out of the window. In fact, anything to pass the time until he could shut down his terminus and go home to vegetate on the settee while he watched stupid, boring programmes on his ancient black and white TV.

Suffice to say that Dave did *not* have an interesting life.

Why? Because he had no money. With a pile of money he could have a fast car with a go faster stripe along the side. With a pile of money he could go places, buy things and impress lots of scantily dressed women inside an expensive disco club. With a pile of money he could sunbathe on a yacht, his own yacht, and have his high cholesterol meals served to him by some bikini clad beauty that he had met in some far off country.

He sighed. These were just pipedreams. Fantasies. Dreams that he never hoped to fulfill.

Dave had worked hard in his university days. After achieving a first in his BSc., he stayed on to get a Masters in his chosen subject, Information Technology & Computer Science. What a waste of money that was… If this job was anything to go by he may as well have spent his money on something more useful, like a better PC screen or a new pair of trainers, or a karaoke machine.

Karaoke. Now there was something he could do… A karaoke DJ and presenter.

'*Nah!*' he thought, '*It means working into the early hours and I'd lose my sleep.*'

Dave wasn't married. He wasn't interested in being married. Too many screaming kids - one kid is too many! - and a whining, possessive wife who would spend all his money on clothes that she never wore and cook the same, repetitive meals every day. No, marriage is definitely not for him.

However, thirty year old Dave just had to get himself out of this rut. He went on-line to look for a course that would appeal to him and make his day a little more interesting. He found one. A home study degree course in Creative Technology. That will do. It'll fill the time in nicely. He could study while answering mindless, stupid helpline questions or while watching the TV. After all, multi-tasking is easy with a brain like Dave's.

Twelve months later, Dave added a second Bsc. to the framed certificates on his lounge wall. Now he could do something interesting, like invent and compile a computer game. If it was a good game, perhaps it would attract some interest and earn him some big money.

Attract interest, it did!

After spending six months writing and developing the game he set up a web site and posted the game on-line. With his meagre savings spent on publicity, incoming subscriptions for the game, initially, were few and far between but Dave hung on in there in the hopes that uptake on the game would improve.

After a while Dave began to lose all hope of the game being popular when it was flagged up to Satan's attention. Here was something Satan could use for his own benefit. With a little intervention from him the game could send some business in his direction.

*

Dave woke up one morning, rubbed the sleep from his eyes, washed and dressed, and then boiled water for his usual breakfast of strong coffee with three spoons of sugar. He didn't eat much, but when he did have a meal it was usually something calorific and low in nutrients.

As he waited for the kettle to boil he couldn't help thinking what a strange dream he had had, last night.

He had dreamt that he had 'done a deal with the Devil.' A pact. A contract between Satan and himself. The dream was so vivid that Dave sat at the kitchen table and wrote down what he had dreamt about.

There were just seven conditions in this contract:

1. Satan will make the game successful and allow Dave to keep all income from it if,

2. Dave will post a four million pound prize on-line to entice players to take part.

3. Satan will ensure that nobody is left to cash in the prize pot if,

4. All final eight Avatars are eliminated and,

5. All of the final eight Avatar owners' lives are extinguished.
6. If any of the players evade death in real life, for any reason, Dave will have to take their place in

the queue for entrance through the gates to Hades.

7. All the aforementioned game conditions had to be fulfilled for the game to finish.

'A strange dream,' Dave thought. *'Make the game successful then kill off all the players? Oh, well. It was only a dream, wasn't it? A weird dream, but a dream, nonetheless.'*

A strange dream, indeed... Or was it real? Had he really made a deal with the Devil?

Dave attached his notes to the fridge door with a magnet and went to the bus stop to await his palatial carriage to his dreary workplace.

*

Each night, on returning home to his PC console, he logged into the game's admin page to see how his game was faring in the world of PC games. As the weeks turned into months Dave watched his income gradually increase. He would soon have enough to buy a new TV - a colour Smart HDTV with a handset that would enable him to change channels without having to get off the settee. He put a reminder in his brain's memory bank to go down town to get one in a couple of days.

A surprising thing then happened.

Arriving home, one evening, he noticed that the game was taking off. Subscription levels shot up and people started to send word round their social media pages about 'what a fantastic game' it was. A 'must have' for all gamers, with a life-changing prize for anyone good enough to win. After several months, he was two hundred million pounds richer!

Dave started to read up on yachts and foreign climes. He resigned from his tedious job and started to spend, spend, spend. Life, for him couldn't have turned out better. He travelled to many of the places he could previously only dream of and he now had a whole queue of gorgeous girls - some bikini clad - following him around, vying for his attention.

In time, he forgot about his pact with the Devil.

*

There was now just one last player's life for Satan to "help" to expire.

What Satan didn't realise, however, was that that last player was unknowingly planning to throw a curved ball at him. A curved ball just like the one that had been launched at him several months ago. A curved ball that would, again create the blue screen of death to appear on his database screen…

EPILOGUE

It has been said that 'Greed is the driver of success.'

Is that true? Well, yes, but not entirely. Not all successful people are greedy, but let's face it, one *has* to have some inclination to be selfish to succeed, and in many cases greed is an overriding factor in any selfish motive, isn't it? People 'get what they can' out of life without giving anything back. Isn't that selfish? Isn't that bordering on greedy? Who knows…?

Many months ago, eight people started playing a game that could net any one of them a cool four million pounds if he or she won. It had cost each player a few hundred pounds to play, but do you think those eight players would have dedicated so much time, effort and money to a game that didn't have *any* reward? I doubt it.

Anyway, those final eight players, the ones who had succeeded in reaching the final three rounds of the game, had no idea that David Smithers - Dave to his mates - had done a 'get rich quick' deal with the devil, and clause 5 of Dave's contract with Satan stipulated all players should die.

The contract was for eight people to die, and Satan was going to make sure that eight people died!

*

Sister Gracey was called to Mother Superior's office.

She had an inclination about what Mother Superior wanted to speak to her about and she drew a deep breath before lightly tapping on the door and waiting for the command to enter.

"Come in," invited Mother Superior.

Gracey entered the room and stood in front of Mother Superior's desk.

"You called me to your office, Reverend Mother?"

"Yes, Sister Gracey. I have been told that you play internet games at night instead of resting," Mother superior replied, looking sternly over the top of her spectacles.

No response. Gracey merely looked down at the floor in embarrassment.

"Well, Sister Gracey? Have you?"

"Yes," Gracey whispered without looking up.

"You know that it is against our guidelines to play internet games... Any games, especially when you should be resting. You know that you need to awaken early to be able to prepare the morning breakfasts? How can you carry out your duties proficiently if you are contantly tired?"

"Has there been a complaint made against me?" Gracey asked, looking at Mother Superior with disappointment on her face.

"No there hasn't, but that's not the point," Mother Superior barked. "Why do you keep breaking our rules so flagrantly, Gracey? Is your life here so bad that you need to find distractions from other places?"

"No, no. I love my job and I love my life here."

"So, why do you feel the need to make your life better. What is it that your life is lacking? Perhaps there is something I can do to make your life better fulfilled?"

"You don't need to do anything…"

There was a pause while Gracey thought of the words she could use to persuade Mother Superior of her motives and intentions.

"Brother Gilbert told me of an opportunity that I could consider, to do things for the good of our convent. He told me about an on-line game that pays out four million pounds to the winner. He persuaded me that that amount of money would surely make our lives here much more comfortable. He said that we could have more bankets for the winter time, or air conditioning to cool us in the summer, or better equipment to manage our gardens. He even gave me the moey for the entrance fee. Please believe me when I say that my motives were purely selfless. My intention is to help a lot of good causes and, perhaps, improve our lives here…"

Gracey's words tailed off to silence as she waited for Mother Superior to speak.

"What do you mean, your intention *is* to help a lot of good causes?" asked Mother Superior, with a hint of puzzlement.

"I won the game Reverend Mother!" delared Gracey, a huge smile adorning her face. "I have four million pounds in my bank account that we can use for good causes... All of it... Every penny! We can do so much good with this money."

And there it is... Another curved ball heaved at Entity.

*

Satan had been following Sister Gracey's incredible path throughout the game, and he suspected that she was being helped to win the game. There was only one other entity that could prevent Gracey from being killed... And we all know who that entity is - Satan's nemesis, God.

God knew that Gracey was a good person and a good nun. He knew that her motives and intentions were utterly selfless, and he just had to make sure that she was able to fulfill the most desired wish in all her life - to help people without considering what the consequences of her actions could do to herself.

Satan spat fire in anger. He threw things. He kicked things - especially any unfortunate idiot that got in his way while waiting in the queue to enter the gates of Hades. He was enraged when he realised what had happened. He knew that he was unable to do anything about God's intervention and he crashed around Hades looking for anything, or anyone, to burn. There will now be a good many people living a life of hell… In Hell! Satan could do nothing to stop his screens from turning blue again.

But what of clause six in the contract with Dave? If Sister Gracey was destined to live, as decreed by God, himself, Dave must now take her place in Hades.

Let us return to the convent…

*

Mother Superior didn't know what to say to Sister Gracey. Her jaw had dropped down and was now resting on her chest. Her eyes were as wide as dinner plates and her mind had gone into overdrive as it bounced around the inside of her head, trying to comprehend Gracey's last words.

Gracey spoke first, to break the silence that had descended on the room.

"So I'll go and make a list of good causes that we can spend the money on, shall I?"

Mother Superior just nodded in silence as Gracey turned and made her way to the door, smiling from ear-to-ear.

A few days later Mother Superior and Sister Gracey together agreed on the list of good causes :

- Books for a local children's school.
- Famine relief for a war torn country.
- Installation of communal water taps in a far-off drought ridden country.
- Upgrade of equipment at the local hospital.

Anything left was spent on making life at the convent a little more comfortable for the nuns.

Air conditioning was high on this list, followed closely by winter blankets and gardening equipment. A selfish move? No. More like a gift donated by a nun and graciously accepted by another nun.

*

Sister Gracey was, once more, called to Mother Superior's office.

"Sister Gracey, do you have the time to go and help Brother François to administer the last rites to some poor soul who is about to die at the hospital?"

"Yes, Of course. Is the person anyone we know?"

"No. He is an Englishman who was taking a holiday here, in Monaco, and he apparantly had an accident in his kitchen. That's all I know, but you'll be able to get better details from Brother François. Hurry now, or Brother François will be too late to administer the last rites."

Gracey hurried down to her cell to pack an overnight bag in case her hospital visit lasted longer than one day. She hurried down to the shiny new van that she had bought for the convent, a smile on her face. Perhaps she will have time to visit Brother Gilbert's cell, once more, to make sure his injuries were healing properly and catch up on some longed for 'attention' that she sorely missed…

She drove to the village hospital where Brother François was waitig for her, standing next to the entrance door lazily strumming a guitar.

"Hurry, Sister Gracey. The man is in a bad way and he doesn't have very much longer to live."

They both hurried to the ward where the tourist had been bedded down. Gracey looked down at the patient and saw how pale and wan his expression was.

"Hello," she said to him, "I'm Sister Gracey. I've come to see how you are. Do you need anything to make you comfortable?" she asked.

The man looked back with half closed eyes. Eyes that painted a bleak picture of the man's last minutes on this earth and of his future.

"No, I'm fine, thank you," he whispered.

"Tell Brother François what your name is. Do you know why we have come to your bedside?"

"My name is Dave Smithers. Are you an angel? You look like one"

Gracey and François smiled down at Dave.

Dave's life faded from him as Brother François voiced the last rites.

*

One month earlier.

After Gracey had banked her winnings, Dave had decided to moor his yacht in the coastal town of Monaco-Ville. The Monaco Grand Prix was taking place and he thought it a good time to visit France and hear the roar of the formula one cars as they shot past the harbour.

He had sat on the viewing deck of his palatial yacht, enjoying the sun, the scenery and the noise of the racing cars. At lunch time he had gone below to make himself and his tanned, bikini clad "friend", a sandwich and a pot of coffee. He needn't have done that because his companion had offered to do it for him, but he wanted to stretch his legs, so he bid her to "… stay there. I'll do it."

In the galley, as he prepared the sandwiches, Satan saw an opportunity to invoke clause six.

Dave had reached into the cupboard directly in front of him to take out a couple of plates for the snacks, but he had failed to close the cupboard door tightly against its magnetised door stop. He had accidentally knocked the butter knife onto the floor from the work top. The exact same moment that he had bent down to pick up the knife, the yacht had yawed slightly as a passing cruiser's wash lapped against the yacht's hull. Dave hadn't noticed the cupboard door swing open as the boat rolled.

Standing up to finish preparing the snacks he had bashed the back of his head on the corner of the open cupboard door. His female companion had come down to see what the loud bang was. Dave turned to look at her and that was the last time, ever, that he saw a bikini clad beauty. He dropped to the floor and blood oozed from his head wound, staining the carpet adjacent to his head a deep red colour.

Dave was airlifted to a little village hospital in Carros, a few miles from Manaco-Ville, and about three miles from a convent. There was no room at the main hospital in Monaco city, but his injury was so bad that the medics had considered it to be fatal so they had taken him to the nearest place that he could be made comfortable until his final ending.

*

Dave Smithers no longer exists in the real world. His luck had finaly run out and he had died in order to take the place of someone who is kind, and generous and selfless... And alive.

The next time you make a wish, be careful what you wish for or you might wish that you hadn't made that wish.

Dave made a wish during his sleep, one night. He wished that he could be filthy rich and suddenly he was. Look where that got him... He can't even enjoy the fruits of his wish now.

He has to put up with being bullied and abused and kicked and shouted at by Satan and he doesn't even have any air conditioning to cool his sweated brow.

Satan still hasn't fixed his blue screens, but when he does... Watch yourself!

BOOKS BY THE AUTHOR

MY ROGUE GENE
ISBN: 978-1-80074-296-3

Olympia Publishers
Amazon Bookstore

Bill's autobiography. Full of amusing anecdotes from his past, from the time he was born right up to the time he left the army after twelve years service.

MY GROWN-UP ROGUE GENE
ISBN: 978-1-80439-313-0

More nonsense from Bill's rogue gene, now grown-up and still interfering with Bill's life.
This is a sequel to *My Rogue Gene*, highlighting Bill's life from the time he left the army to his life in civvy street and into retirement.

Olympia Publishers
Amazon Bookstore

BEHIND ROSE BORDERED WINDOWS
ISBN - 979-1-22014-338-7

Winner of the Golden Book Special Prize at the Rome Literary Awards 2024

William Colbert's wife dies. Everyone is convinced her death was an accident, including William, until the cause of her death is called into question.

He has inherited a country manor in a remote part of the country, well away from all his memories of a once idyllic marriage. But his new life is thrown into disarray when he witnesses distressing events through the windows of the five picture postcard cottages facing his new home... Nobody believes what he has seen, until the truth about his inheritance is revealed.

Europe Books
Amazon Bookstore

europe books